WANT FREE STUFF?

CHARACTER INTERVIEWS?

ACTIVITY SHEETS?

SHORT STORIES?

DISCOUNTED BOOKS?

OTHER BONUSES?

C.T.'S MONTHLY NEWSLETTER?

OF COURSE, YOU DO!

ctwalsh.fun/msmbonuses

VALENTINE'S DUH

MIDDLE SCHOOL MAYHEM: BOOK SEVEN

C.T. WALSH

FARCICAL PRESS

COVER CREDITS

Cover design by Books Covered
Cover photographs © Shutterstock
Cover illustrations by Maeve Norton

For my Family

Thank you for all of your support

1
___

Amor. Love. The strongest human emotion. Well, except the fear you have after you eat tacos and really have to go to the bathroom and you're not sure if you'll make it to said bathroom. But we're talking about love. Tacos may or may not come into play in this story, so let's stick to the main topic, okay?

There's no situation that creates more mayhem in a middle school student's life than romance. And Valentine's Day is the apex. Add in a full moon and things get downright hairy. Not werewolf hairy, but close. And the situation at Cherry Avenue Middle School fit that description like a glove. And don't worry. There's a whole lot more to this story than a bunch of gooey love. I can't tell you exactly what just yet. You'll just have to trust me on this.

It was a Friday afternoon in late January. I was with my crew that consisted of my girlfriend, Sophie, my best friend, Ben, Luke, Just Charles, and Cheryl Van-Snoogle Something at Frank's Pizza, our favorite spot to hang out. Frank's had the best pizza around and was within walking distance of school. A lot of kids typically met up there and that day it was downright packed.

As we chowed down, Cheryl looked casually at Just Charles (Call him Charlie or Chuck. I dare you!) and asked, "What's the plan for the 14th?" She was Just Charles' girlfriend of a few months and she was referring to the momentous occasion in most middle schoolers' lives: Valentine's Day.

Just Charles thought about it for a minute. "What is that? A Friday?"

"Yeah," Cheryl said, monotone.

Just Charles continued, "I don't know. I'll probably just eat pizza, chips, and watch Robot Wars."

"Oh..." Cheryl said, disappointed.

I looked at Just Charles and mouthed, "The dance, bro. The dance."

Just Charles nodded and said, "I'll be wearing pants, though."

Ugh. I mouthed again, "The dance."

"Oh, the dance," Just Charles said. "What dance? Oh, the dance," he said, a lightbulb flashing above his head. He looked at Cheryl and asked, "Do you want to go with me?"

"Sure," Cheryl said, unenthused.

"Nice one, Romeo," Luke whispered.

I leaned in and asked Sophie, "You want to go, right?" It was real smooth.

"I definitely want to go. And I really want to win Cupid's Cutest Couple Contest. I heard about it on the radio."

"I heard about that, too," Ben said. "The winner gets a dance hosted by DJ Fight Club."

"Along with Calvin Conklin and Devi Divine as the MCs," Sophie said.

"I love her, but he's an idiot," Cheryl said.

Calvin Conklin was a local newscaster who had tried to ruin my life on a few occasions. In his defense, it wasn't on purpose. He was just an idiot, as Cheryl said.

Sophie looked at me with puppy dog eyes and asked, "Can you help me win?"

"Well, I'm super cute, so that should do it, no?" I said.

"It's a radio call-in contest, so unfortunately, your cuteness won't come into play," Sophie said with a smile.

"But do we really want to win a contest that brings Calvin to our school dance? That has disaster written all over it," I said.

"He's not that bad," Sophie said.

"He didn't mistake *you* for being a time traveler. I still have people come up to me in public and ask me for the winning lottery numbers."

"Please," Sophie asked. "I really want this."

"Okay," I said. How could I say no to Sophie?

Sophie looked at me and said, "I didn't tell you about the really good part. Not only do we get the party, but we get a limo, backstage passes to Goat Turd- they're huge now after the whole Halloween dance thing. And dinner at Le Fort."

"Le Fart?" I asked.

The girls just shook their heads. Ben, Luke, and Just Charles, of course, laughed.

Cheryl ignored my awesome joke and said, "That sounds amazing."

"Goat Turd owes me big, by the way," I said. We got them to go viral on YouTube. It was just a normal Friday night.

"Owes us," Ben corrected. "We all helped."

"Definitely," I said.

"I'll bring a new lady friend," Luke added.

"What happened to Jasmine Jane?" Ben asked.

"I don't want to talk about it," Luke said, staring at the mesmerizing sauce atop his half-eaten slice of pizza.

"She dumped you?" I asked.

"It was mutual," Luke said, defensively.

"So, you got dumped?" Ben asked, smiling.

"We broke up. That's all you need to know."

"Have some pizza, bro," I said. "It always makes people feel better after getting dumped."

"I didn't get dumped," Luke said, sheepishly.

Sophie looked at Ben and said, "What do you think about all of this? The Valentine's Day dance is a big deal. Especially if we win the contest and have DJ Fight Club there."

Ben took a deep breath. "It's shameless corporatism. I'm not participating. The whole thing is a scam cooked up by florists, jewelry stores, chocolatiers, and greeting card companies."

"That's a pretty big conspiracy, dude," Just Charles said.

"That's what people who can't get dates say," Luke said.

"Oh, really?" Ben asked.

"Uh, yeah. It's on Wikipedia," Luke said.

"Is it really?" Cheryl asked. She was a journalist for the Gopher Gazette, our middle school newspaper. Once you cite a source, she'll believe whatever you tell her.

"There's nobody out there for me," Ben said.

"Of course, there is," Sophie said.

"Do you think I haven't looked?" Ben said, throwing the crust of his pizza down onto his plate.

Luke looked across the restaurant and said, "Who. Is. That?" His eyes looked like they were going to pop out of his head and onto the pizza tray. I loved exotic toppings on my pizza, but that was not one I was looking forward to trying.

We all looked in the same direction. I had no idea who the girl was that he was looking at.

Ben whispered, "It's her."

"Who?" I asked.

"The one," he said, simply.

I ran my hand in front of Ben's eyes. He didn't even blink. I said, "Boo!" He didn't budge.

Luke asked again, "Who is that?"

Sophie said, "That's Allie Larkin."

"That's Allison Larkin?" I asked.

Ben said, "But. But. But. She had braces."

Luke added, "And zits."

Just Charles frowned and said, "Glasses, too. She looks so different."

"Who? How? Why? When?" Luke said.

That's the thing about middle school. One day you could

look around the school and not see anyone that catches your eye and then the next moment, a caterpillar with zits and crooked glasses turns into a beautiful butterfly and floats right through the air in front of you. The only problem? That beautiful butterfly that was Allie Larkin just floated in front of both Ben and Luke.

2

I sat with Ben and Just Charles in my basement, as we strategized about how to win Cupid's Cutest Couple Contest for Sophie. I needed their help to make it all work. Luke usually just messed these things up, so he wasn't invited.

I looked at the two of them and said, "There's a lot riding on this, boys. Just Charles is in the dog house with Cheryl and Sophie really wants this. And don't forget, Ben may have found the future Mrs. Gordon."

"Did not," Ben said, defensively. "Maybe. Probably."

"Let's put our heads together. Pizza's on the way. Just Charles, try not to get too crazy with the sugar. The last thing we need is Evil Chuck getting too wild."

"Understood. He's not always so bad, is he?"

"Not always. There's a time and a place," I said, smiling. If you haven't met Evil Chuck, you will. He's not so bad, but you'll just have to see for yourself. "So, how do you win a call-in contest? How can we get an advantage?"

"All I got is redial," Ben said. "Just keep pressing it."

"Everybody's got that," Just Charles said. "What about a robo dialer?"

"Like the cold callers trying to sell you timeshares or get you to donate all your stuff?"

"Those are so annoying. I get so many stupid phone calls," Ben said.

"Me, too. Well, let's use it to our benefit. But how?" I asked.

"We can try to buy one. How much do you think they cost?" Just Charles said.

I fired up my iPad and searched Google. An eBay listing came up showing an automatic dialer.

"Here's one for fifty bucks," I said.

"Fifty bucks?" Just Charles yelled.

"What? That's crazy," Ben added.

These poor guys just didn't understand the ladies.

I waved off their concerns. "I can use my birthday money for that. Sophie's worth it."

"Don't you think other people might try to do that, too?" Ben asked.

"Yeah, if it's only fifty bucks," Just Charles added.

Ben said, "It's a pretty big contest. They've been advertising it for a while."

"You might be right." I thought for a minute. "But what other people probably don't have is a team working together."

"What does that do for us?" Just Charles asked.

"No idea," I said, chuckling.

My mother called down the stairs into the basement, "Austin, come grab the pizza."

"You have thirty seconds to figure something out," I said, hopping up and heading over to the stairs.

I came back holding a steaming box of pizza from

Frank's. It was a glorious sight and we hadn't even opened it yet. I put the box down on the table and tossed plates at the boys.

"What do we got?" Just Charles asked.

I opened the box and said, "Half meatball. Half eggplant."

"I'm in love," Just Charles said, grabbing a meatball slice.

"Don't let Cheryl hear you say that or you'll be in the dog house forever," I said.

"This conversation is off the record, just so you know," Just Charles said.

"Come to papa," Ben said, sliding an eggplant slice onto his plate.

I grabbed a slice. "So, what did you come up with?" I asked, laughing.

"So, we've got a crew of people, one robo dialer, and a dream," Ben said.

"We've only got one phone line and a robo dialer. What good is a network of people?" I asked.

"It doesn't sound all that good," Just Charles said, frowning.

"But what if those people had computers that we could network together?" I said.

"What are you thinking?" Just Charles asked.

"I'm thinking I would like to eat two slices at the same time," Ben said, adding a meatball slice to the eggplant slice already on his plate.

"Power move, bro," I said. "But we gotta get down to business. What if somehow we could use a bunch of computers that use voice over IP for their phone service and connect it to the robo dialer?" I asked.

"We could write some code to use the dialer on everyone's phone and we could repeatedly blast the radio's call-in line," Just Charles said, tapping his chin.

"This could be our headquarters. We can pull ten phone lines here to this one," I said, pointing to our house phone. "Then all we have to do is get the trivia question right."

"I can write a program to do that," Just Charles said. "Well..."

"Well, what?" I asked.

"Evil Chuck might have to make an appearance. We're short on time. We're gonna have to build this at warp speed." Evil Chuck was Just Charles' alter ego that was triggered by massive amounts of sugar.

I looked at Ben and asked, "You have any thoughts?"

"Oh, sorry. Was just zoning out, thinking about Allie."

"You really like her?" I asked, surprised.

"I don't even know her, but I keep thinking about her." He waved me off. "It's not a big deal."

"You sure about that?" Just Charles asked.

"Well, I might want to ask her to the Valentine's dance," Ben said with a shrug.

"No big deal? When was the last girl you wanted to go out with?" I asked, my voice rising two octaves.

"Mildred Byrnes," Ben said.

"Your babysitter?"

"She was some woman. Millie's in college now. Do you think she'll go with me?"

I laughed. "Umm, no. I thought you liked Allie?"

"Oh, yeah. Totally."

◇

THE NEXT MORNING, we headed into school on the bus. I was sitting in the aisle seat with Ben to my right and Sammie in the aisle seat opposite me. Ben leaned forward and called across to Sammie.

"Hey, Sammie? Do you think you could help me? I want to ask Allie to the dance."

"Umm, sure. Yeah, absolutely," she said. I think she was a little surprised, to be honest.

"What about me?" I asked.

"What do you know about asking girls out?" Ben asked.

"Have you met Sophie?" Sammie asked. "She's way out of his league." She looked at me and said, "No offense."

"None taken. I agree with you. Just don't tell her," I said with a smile.

Ben looked at me and said, "I was there when you asked her out. I was not all that impressed."

"That's a fair point you make, Benjamin. But you have to admit, I'm the poster boy for having a girlfriend out of my league."

"You think Allie's out of my league?" Ben asked, nervously.

"No, I just meant that I'm the Harry Potter of asking girls out."

"You sure you didn't slip her a love potion?" Ben asked.

"That *was* some powerful magic you pulled off," Sammie added.

"He fell flat on his face while we were running on the track. It was the worst move I've ever seen," Ben said.

"What can I say? It's part of my charm." I looked at Sammie and asked, "Who are you going with?"

"I'm not going with anyone. I want to go by myself."

"Really? Why?" Ben asked.

"After being all crazy about Randy and Derek, I just want to have fun with my friends." Sammie changed the subject. "So, the first order of business for you is letting Allie know that you exist."

"I talked to her in elementary school. We were friends," Ben said.

"What grade was that?" I asked, my brow furrowed.

"Second."

"That was five years ago, dude."

"She's in my art class."

"Do you talk to her?" Sammie asked.

"No, she's on the other side of the room."

Sammie said, "Well, make some eye contact with her across the room. Stare at her for a few seconds longer than you should. And when she looks at you, smile. Count to three. And then go back to your art project."

"Are you closer to the door or is she?" I asked.

"I am. Why?" Ben asked.

I needed to prove my value to this mission. "Okay, so stall and wait for her to pass you on the way out. Say hi."

Ben was busy texting on his phone like a mad man.

"What are you doing?" I asked. I was dropping all of this phenomenal wisdom and he wasn't even paying attention. Harry Potter didn't have to deal with that kind of nonsense. When the Chosen One spoke, people listened.

"I'm writing this down. This is gold, Sammie."

I scoffed. "What about my stuff?"

"Oh, yours, too," Ben said, but seemingly not as excited as he was before.

"If you're feeling bold, why not throw out a wink?" I added.

"I can't do that. Would you have winked at Sophie?" Ben asked.

"Of course not. I nearly wet my pants when I first met her. But we're talking about you."

"I don't have the confidence to pull off an unsolicited wink." Ben looked down at his pants. "I think I may have just tinkled right now."

"Ugh. I know you're joking, but ugh. You just gotta be cool," Sammie said.

"Yeah, girls like the strong, silent type," I said.

"We definitely wish some of you would be more silent," Sammie said, looking at me.

"Hey!" I shook my head and turned back to Ben. "Throw out a nod and a yo, and you'll be good to go."

"I'm not a rapper, dude. I can't just throw a yo and be good to go. But, should I write her a rap?"

Sammie and I both said, "No!"

"You can't wink unsolicited, but you're going to rap for her?"

"Good point," Ben said, scratching his head.

"Baby steps, Ben. We'll get you there," Sammie said with a smile. I wasn't so sure.

~

JUST CHARLES CAME over that night after we were both done with homework and each night after that until the contest. We had to code our butts off to win this contest for Sophie. We were in my basement, both sitting in front of laptops. I was working on some research, trying to figure out how to hack the robo dialer. I had already ordered it and it was only two days away from arriving. We wouldn't have much time to get it all to work, though, as the contest call-in was only four days away.

Just Charles was busy writing code to connect all of the computer networks together so we could turn the one robo dialer into ten robo dialers and control them all from one location; my phone. The Bat Phone. It was that serious. And powerful. True, when we called it, Calvin Conklin would be showing up to our dance and not Batman, but still.

It was going to be tight, but we weren't going all out just yet. I was still rationing Just Charles' sugar intake. One soda per hour plus one snack or pizza slice. It seemed to be a perfect balance of supercharging his brain and coding power without turning him into Evil Chuck, the maniacal evil genius that turned full sentences into one jumbled word. He operated that fast. I would save that in case we needed it.

"Did I tell you that I figured out an algorithm for popularity?" Just Charles asked. "It can rank each kid based on certain inputs and give recommendations on which areas to focus on for maximum popularity improvement."

"Sounds interesting."

"I came out dead last," Just Charles said. "Well, without dating Cheryl. With Cheryl, I'm in the middle of the pack."

"There are some intriguing applications there, for sure, but we need to get this project done, before I get dumped and I come out dead last in popularity."

"Yep. Working on it," Just Charles said, typing away into his laptop. His fingers were moving like lightning strikes across the keyboard.

~

WE KEPT at it for the next few nights. It was Friday night. We had the robo dialer and had a solid eighteen hours until the contest. Twelve if you accounted for some sleep. And maybe a little more if we could work on separate areas of code at the same time. We hadn't resorted to that just yet.

Just Charles was coding away in my basement. He said,

"Hey, did I tell you about my algorithm that can predict your popularity?"

"Yes. Can it predict my popularity if I don't win this contest for Sophie?"

"You don't need it for that. It's the same as mine without Cheryl. Bottom of the barrel."

"Funny. Why are you calculating your popularity without Cheryl? Things going okay?"

"Well, she's still mad at me. Plus, things have been a little blah lately. I think Cheryl and I just need to rekindle the flame."

"You've only been dating for three months! How could your flame be unkindled?" I wasn't convinced that was a word, but I knew he would understand it.

"That's like four years in dog years."

"That seems like an appropriate comparison. I'm sure she would appreciate it."

"I mean, I don't know what the heck I did wrong. I didn't know my calendar by memory. Next month's calendar, for that matter. Am I supposed to know what I'm doing on every day for the next three months? A year?"

"I hear ya, dude. You never know what they're gonna get you on. You gotta be prepared for anything. Love is war, bro." I thought that maybe that should be the title of a song for our band.

"It sure is."

"How much more do you think we have to do?" I asked.

"We're halfway there. Maybe."

Ugh. I wasn't sure we were gonna finish. But I was sure that I would get dumped if I messed this all up. No pressure. Sophie was just the love of my life. If love is war, I was going to lose the war if we didn't get to finish this robo dialer on steroids before the contest. And time was running out.

3

J ust Charles ended up sleeping over. We coded for half the night and then slept for five or so hours. I at least made it to the couch. Just Charles passed out right at the table. When I woke him up, he had half a slice of pizza stuck to his face.

"What's going on? Where am I?" Just Charles asked, pulling the slice of pizza off his face. He looked at the slice and said, "Oh, sweet. Breakfast," and took a bite.

I looked at my phone. We had six hours until the contest.

"What else do we have to get done?" I asked.

Just Charles took a minute to scan his laptop. "We've got more code to write. And I have to erase seventeen thousand lines of v's and c's. Apparently, half my face was on the keyboard and the other half was on breakfast when I fell asleep."

"Should I call Evil Chuck?" I asked. I knew what he would say, since I think he kinda liked him.

"I think you have to."

"I'm not sure my mother will let us have soda at ten o'clock in the morning, but give me a few minutes," I said, heading upstairs in stealth mode.

Within an hour, Just Charles had ingested enough sugar to power a rocket ship to Mars. He was coding in hyperspeed. I was concerned the six sodas were too much and that my mother would wonder why the heck he kept running to the bathroom. But we were clearly making progress.

Finally, Evil Chuck pushed back from the table and said at superspeed, "Sendthislinktoeverone. It'll get thephonesystemsetup."

"Okay, dude. Great job. We still have to configure the dialer, right? And wean you off the sugar."

"Noyouwillnot!" Evil Chuck yelled, slamming his fist down on the table. A can of soda tipped over and spilled. Evil Chuck put his face to the table and starled licking it.

"I've created a monster," I said to myself, shaking my head.

❧

WE ONLY HAD an hour before everyone showed up and two hours before the contest started. The crew had started to arrive.

"Hey!" I said. I may have been a little bit sugared up, too.

"How's it going? I'm so excited. We're gonna win, right?" Sophie asked.

"I hope so. This thing will give us a huge advantage," I said, patting the Bat Phone, "but we can't hack the whole thing. We can't control how many other people participate or what they do to get through." I mean, I guess we could've knocked out satellites and cell towers, but I think that would've been a touch overboard. And a bit out of our league. Even for Evil Chuck's destructive side.

I looked toward the stairs as Ben and Sammie arrived, but was distracted by Evil Chuck.

Evil Chuck had a soda in each hand and was going from one to the other, chugging them back and forth.

"Evil Chuck, no! Where did you get that?" I yelled. He must've found the secret stash that I was hiding from him and saving for when the party started.

Evil Chuck crushed the cans in his hands and tossed them over his shoulders. They hit the wall behind him with a clank as he yelled, "Whatsupeverbody? It'sgonnabeaspectacularday. Ithinkwecanwinthewholething, dontchaknow?"

"What the heck is going on with Charles?" Sophie asked, her eyes wide in shock.

"Oh, you've never met Evil Chuck. This is Just Charles consuming a month's worth of sugar in a few hours. It gives him super powers, but he also cannot be contained."

I turned around and Just Charles was gone!

"Where the heck did he go?"

I heard a commotion by the stairs and looked to find Luke tumbling down them, eventually crashing into the wall with a bang and a groan.

Sammie rushed over to him first. "What happened? Are you okay?"

"I think Evil Chuck escaped," he said, gasping for air.

"He didn't tell me how to connect the network to the robo dialer!" I yelled, heading for the stairs. "We need to capture Evil Chuck!"

"Dead or alive!" Luke yelled.

"We need him alive, idiot!" Ben yelled.

"Oh, right," Luke said, following us up the stairs. "But it was just fun saying it."

We followed the maniacal laughter out the back door, which he left wide open. The laughter continued outside, but we couldn't figure out from where. I turned around in a circle as the laughter encircled us. I looked up to see Just Charles in our old tree house.

"He's up there!" I yelled.

"He pulled up the ladder," Ben said. "How're we gonna get up there?"

"Does your dad have a chainsaw?" Luke asked.

"We're not chopping down the tree, idiot. We need him alive, remember?"

"Oh, right," Luke said, scratching his head.

"No, I'm with Luke," Sophie said. "Chop it down! We're too close!"

The clock was ticking. We needed to come up with something fast. He had the upper hand. There was no way we could storm his fort and take him hostage. We were gonna have to persuade him to come out.

I took a deep breath and said, "I hate to do this, but I have an idea. It might make things worse after the contest, but it should get him down."

"What is it?" Sophie asked.

I told them the plan. Ben and Luke hustled back inside and retrieved a box of pizza and as many cans of soda they could carry.

"He might be crashing. I hope he doesn't pass out up there," I said.

I grabbed a soda can from Ben and popped the top. As soon as the carbonation released with a pop, Just Charles' head peeked over the side wall of the tree house.

"Whatwasthat?" he asked. "EvilChucklikeysodapop!"

"We have pizza, too, Evil Chuck!" Luke yelled, while opening the pizza box.

Evil Chuck was on his feet as the steam from the hot pizza hit the cool air.

"We need to contain him," I said. I handed the open soda can to Sophie and said, "I'll be right back."

I ran into the garage and returned with a handful of bungee cords and some jumper cables from my dad's car stuff. I dropped it behind a bush and returned to the rest of the crew.

Evil Chuck had dropped the ladder, but hadn't come down yet. He was still tentative.

"Go put that soda down at the bottom of the ladder," I said to Sophie.

Sophie ran over and left the soda can on the grass.

"Okay, Luke. Plate a slice and put that ten feet farther from the soda."

Luke did as he was told.

"Ben, drop those sodas. Ladies, can you take care of the soda and pizza trail?"

"What are you three gonna do?" Sammie asked.

"We need to capture Evil Chuck. We'll circle around the other side of the house. Whistle when he gets to the second slice and we'll rush him and tie him up." I looked at Ben and Luke. "Let's do this."

We grabbed the bungee cords and jumper cables and headed around the front of the house to the opposite gate, coming in behind Evil Chuck.

I heard Sophie call, "Here, Chuckie, Chuckie."

And then a whistle cut through the air. I knew we had to move fast.

I ran around the corner of the house, jumper cables in my hands. The pounding on the ground and wheezing from our non-athletic lungs must've spooked Evil Chuck. He turned around, half a slice of pizza in one hand and a soda in the other. He ran faster than I'd ever seen him run back toward the ladder.

Sophie actually got to him first and was hanging on one of his ankles as he tried to climb back up the ladder. I grabbed his other leg at the same time that Sammie did. We forced Evil Chuck down off the ladder while Ben and Luke wrapped him up in bungee cords.

"WhyyoudoingthistoEvilChuck?"

"It's okay, Chuck!"

Sammie pet Evil Chuck's hair as he raged. He slowly calmed down. as Sammie continued to pet him as we held him down.

"EvilChuckneedsugar," he whined.

We eventually got Evil Chuck to chill and carried him down to the basement. His head may have hit the wall a few times on the way down the stairs and we did drop him once, but he deserved it.

We tossed Evil Chuck onto the couch. I took the jumper cables and used the clamps like a seat belt to keep him anchored to the couch.

"Glad Cheryl didn't witness Evil Chuck," Sophie whispered to me.

"Oh, man. That would be bad."

"Iwantsugarnow! Gimmesugar!"

"Okay, Chuck. Calm down. We'll give you sugar. You just have to tell us how to set up the network to the robo dialer."

"Sugarfirstnowdude!"

Sophie grabbed a can of soda and held it up to Evil Chuck's lips for a quick sip.

"Iwantmore!"

"Sorry, buddy," I said. "You're gonna have to tell us how to set this thing up. We're running out of time. And then we'll give you some pizza."

"Justplugthecablein!"

"What cable?"

"Theoneoverthere!"

His arms were tied down so I had to follow his eyes. I rushed over to the table and saw a cable next to the dialer. I looked at the ends of the cable and used it to connect the dialer and the computer.

As I checked to see if it was all working, Derek walked downstairs with his buddy, Jayden.

"What's going on down here?" Derek asked.

"We're trying to win a radio contest," Sammie said.

Jayden said, "That sounds kinda cool."

Derek countered, "Sounds totally lame."

Jayden changed his mind. "Yeah, totally lame."

Derek looked around. "Umm, why is Just Charles tied up? What kind of weirdos are you?" Derek asked.

"Just take some pizza and leave. I know that's why you're here."

Derek looked at Just Charles and shrugged. "Sorry, dude. Pizza."

"Iwantpizzatoo!"

Sammie grabbed a slice and held it in front of Evil Chuck. He attacked it like a dog attacks a new shoe, trying to tear it apart.

Derek grabbed his pizza and rushed up the stairs. "They're so weird."

"Alright, it's powering up, right on time," I said. "Soph, you wanna do the honors?"

"Sure," she said with a smile. Sophie pressed the power button, which lit up red.

"Okay," Ben said. "I'm streaming the radio station on my phone now. As soon as they give the signal, we'll start calling."

We all cheered, as my laptop screen flashed the word, 'connected'. But it was premature, as everything, including the lit power button, unlit. The whole house went dark with a pop.

I heard Derek whine, "Mom, Austin blew up the house again."

I called upstairs, "Dad! We need you, quick!"

He was downstairs in about thirty seconds. I had already opened the closet that housed the circuit breaker, but knew I would get in trouble if I touched anything.

"We're running out of time!" I yelled.

"Hurry," Ben said. "They just gave the signal. My phone still works."

"Oh, no!" Sophie said, her shoulders slumping.

"Everybody start calling on your cell phone!" I yelled.

Everybody started dialing.

"Busy," Sammie said.

"Me, too," Sophie said, frustrated.

"Keep going," my dad said, as he flipped on the breaker. The lights flicked back on.

I rushed back to the laptop. It didn't reconnect. I flipped the switch on the robo dialer and waited for it to reboot.

"It's ringing!" Sophie yelled. She pressed speaker on the phone.

"Hello!" A voice called through the phone. "You're caller sixty-two. We're looking for one hundred and two. Please try again!"

"Ahhh, farts," I said, looking back at the laptop. "It's connected!" I clicked the button on the program we built. The robo dialer spit out a bunch of noises. It sounded like R2-D2 from Star Wars when he was angry.

"It's working! We just sent ten calls!"

Everyone crowded around me, except for Just Charles, who was struggling to break free on the couch. We let out a collective groan as none of the calls made it through.

"Busy," Ben said.

"Is it over? We lost?" Sammie asked.

"Not yet," I said.

"Notbyalongshot!" Evil Chuck yelled.

"Simmer down, Chuck," Ben said.

"Let this thing do its magic," I said, as the Bat Phone dialed again.

I scanned the list of all the lines. One showed that it was ringing.

"Soph, it's your line!" I said, pressing the speaker phone button on the Bat Phone.

We waited for three rings, but it felt like a million years. And then the phone clicked. At first, I thought we got hung up on, but then we heard the most glorious of noises.

A man's voice said, "Hello! Congratulations, you're caller 102! What's your name?"

We all cheered.

"Whoa! Who am I speaking to? Just pick one person."

I pointed to Sophie.

She said, "Umm, Sophie."

"You sure about that?" the voice on the other line said with a chuckle.

"Yes."

"Where are you calling from?"

"My boyfriend's house."

"Well, Umm Sophie from My Boyfriend's House, are you ready to take a shot at the Cupid's Cutest Couple Contest trivia question?"

"Yes."

"What song was the hit that put Goat Turd on the map?"

Sophie froze and just stared at the phone.

I whispered, "It's my song I wrote it. The video!"

"Two seconds, Umm Sophie from My Boyfriend's House," the voice said.

"Conformity!" Sophie yelled.

"That's right! You are the winner of the Cupid's Cutest Couple Contest!"

Sophie jumped into my arms, which were barely thicker

than fasting toothpicks, meaning within a split second, we were on the floor in a heap.

"We did it!" I yelled.

"You're so amazing!" Sophie shrieked.

Everyone, including my dad, joined us on the floor in a giant pile, celebrating. Well, everyone except for Evil Chuck.

"Overhere! Ineedahighfive! Somebodyhighfivemyface!"

Gladly, bro. Gladly.

"I think we all should do it," Sophie said. "I'm looking forward to it."

"OhnoIthinkImadamistake."

4

Sophie and I waited for Jimmy and Mrs. Trugman in the Atrium before school on Monday morning. My mother had texted Mrs. Trugman the day before, the day after we won the contest. Try to keep up with the timeline, will ya? We were meeting to discuss the particulars of the dance. She wanted more details before moving forward with it.

We sat on one of the benches underneath the dogwood trees when the doors across the Atrium opened up. Sophie popped up like one of the moles in Wack-a-Mole. I hoped we wouldn't be getting smacked down.

"Jimmy told me the good news! You won the big contest. So exciting," Mrs. Trugman said. "Too bad the school will never let you host it."

Sophie gasped, and her face dropped. She grabbed my arm to steady herself.

"Are you okay?" I asked.

"Oh, hunny. I'm so sorry. I was just kidding. We're a go! The dance is put on by the PTA, so we'll do it in place of our normal Valentine's Day dance. And it will save us money. And we get Goat Turd."

"You like Goat Turd?" I asked, surprised.

"Cameron Quinn is my forever love," Mrs. Trugman said, clutching her heart.

"Mom!" Jimmy yelled. "What about Dad?"

"Oh, yeah. Him, too."

"We don't actually get Goat Turd," Sophie said, trying to break the news gently. "We get DJ fight club for the dance. Austin and I get Goat Turd for winning."

"Oh," Mrs. Trugman said. "Still, that's pretty awesome," she said, seemingly trying to talk herself into it. "So, leave all the details to me. We'll set up the interview with Calvin Conklin as soon as possible."

"Wait. What?" I asked.

"Oh, you didn't know that?" Sophie asked, shrugging super cute-like.

"Seems as if somebody left that one out of the equation," I said, smirking.

"Accidentally," Sophie said, smiling.

"Of course," I said.

"Have a great day, you two. I'll take care of all of this. It's going to be fun!" Mrs. Trugman said with a huge smile.

"Thanks," Sophie said.

Sophie and I headed down the hall toward my locker. The school was still pretty dead. The buses hadn't arrived yet, but there were some before-school activities that were in session.

We stopped at my locker. I dropped my backpack on the floor and grabbed the padlock. I jokingly blocked the dial as I spun in the code.

"Oh, you don't trust me?" Sophie said, laughing.

"You can never be too careful as to who you let know your locker combo. I got Powerlocked the first day last year." True, I was dumb enough to tell my combo to Derek, but still. Lesson learned.

"You don't want to share lockers?" Sophie asked.

"Do you want to share lockers?" It was a big step in a middle school relationship.

"I asked you first."

"I would like that."

"Me, too," Sophie said, smiling.

Noyce. Everything was going great. I won the contest for her. We were going to be Cupid's Cutest Couple, which made her very happy and we were taking our relationship to the next level by sharing locker space. It didn't get any better than that for a nerd like me.

And then I opened my locker and felt something hit me lightly on the foot. I looked down. There was a folded-up piece of notebook paper next to my sneaker.

Sophie leaned down and picked it up.

"What's this?" She was more curious than anything else.

I shrugged. "Don't know. Somebody must've put that in the slot after I left yesterday. Open it up," I said.

Sophie opened the note and started reading, "Valentine's Day is coming up. I know you have a girlfriend." Sophie looked at me and said, "You got that straight, sister." She continued reading, "She seems really sweet and pretty, too." Sophie eyed me. "Again, very true," she said, a little lighter.

"Who is that from?" I asked.

Sophie ignored me and kept reading. "That probably means we'll never be together, but I can't stop myself from trying. I couldn't wait any more to tell you how I feel." Sophie bit her lip and then said, "You should." It was a little more forceful than the last one. She read more, "There's no one like you. You're smart, funny, and nice."

I chimed in, "You got that right, sister."

Sophie smirked at me and continued reading. "I hope to be able to build up the courage to tell you face to face, but until then, I will have to remain your secret admirer."

I just stared at her, not sure how she would react.

"What do you think about that?" Sophie asked, her eyebrow arched seemingly impossibly high.

I said, "It's nice, but I don't care about it."

Sophie handed the note to me like I had just wiped my butt with it. I didn't and I gotta think that would've been painful. I mean, who wants a paper cut, well, there? Not this guy.

"Don't be mad at me," I said. "I didn't write it. I can't help it if I'm irresistible to women." It was a bad joke, I admit.

"It could be Randy pranking you for all we know," Sophie seemed happier to think that was true, rather than the possibility that it could be another girl.

"Oh, thanks. That hurts."

"You know what I mean."

I just let it go. I walked her to her locker, mainly in silence, and dropped her off in time for Advisory. I checked out my potential new locker real estate. It was clean and centrally located. And it meant a deeper relationship with Sophie. I hoped the offer was still on the table after the secret admirer fiasco.

❧

LATER THAT DAY, I sat in English class. Mrs. Conklin was powering through a lesson on love in literature. All of the girls sat on the edges of their seats in rapt attention while most of the dudes were barely holding in their drool. And some of us weren't doing a good job at that.

The Speaker of Doom crackled me out of the daze I was in.

Mrs. Murphy's muffled voice echoed through the concrete classroom, "Mrs. Conklin, please send Austin Davenport down to-"

"The main office," I mocked, completing the sentence.

Mrs. Murphy didn't say that, though. She had said, "the Atrium."

"Huh? What the heck do I need to go to the Atrium for?"

Was this all a set up? Was Principal Buthaire back, lying in wait, ready to duct tape me to the wall? Was Ms. Pierre going to dive out of an air conditioning vent and throw me in the Camel Clutch?

Mrs. Conklin didn't even stop her lesson. I grabbed my stuff and shrugged at everyone who was staring at me. I headed out of the room and down toward the Atrium. I had no idea what was going on. I didn't see anyone else in the hallway, either.

I opened the doors into the Atrium and saw a whole bunch of hustle and bustle not typical while class was in session. And Sophie was front and center to it. She was surrounded by Ms. Pierre, our principal, Mrs. Funderbunk, our music teacher, and Miss Honeywell, who was Mrs. Funderbunk's theatre assistant for all of the school's musicals and plays.

Zorch, the custodian, was sweeping the leaves from beneath the dogwood trees, while Mr. Muscalini shined all of the school's sports trophies.

I walked over to the crowd of ladies without even being

noticed. Miss Honeywell patted Sophie with a makeup brush, while Mrs. Funderbunk fluffed Sophie's curls with her hands.

Ms. Pierre said, "Don't forget, now. There are a lot of great things going on at the school since I took over as principal: the Anne Pierre Leadership Program; the Anne Pierre Aspiring Principal Club; and the Anne Pierre Krav Maga Hybrid Martial Arts Training Program. Not to mention, detentions are down 3% since I took over."

Yeah, after they rose 15,000% under the "leadership" of Prince Butt Hair.

Mrs. Funderbunk was also giving Sophie ideas on what to say. "The eighth-grade interpretation of Romeo and Juliet is set to hit the big Cherry Avenue stage on February 28th. It's going to be huge."

"Yes, but they'll also want to know that after studying the most successful fast-food chains, I implemented a new student drop-off system that reduced morning drop-off times by 17 seconds," Ms. Pierre said.

"Now, you must have proper posture," Mrs. Funderbunk said. "Chin up. Shoulders back. Your right side is your good side, so turn left. Tilt your head. Raise your eyebrow."

"That looks really uncomfortable," I said.

Mrs. Funderbunk looked at me and said, "You of all people should know, Austin, that Mrs. Funderbunk knows posture."

I had no idea why I was supposed to know that, but I wasn't going to try and figure it out.

"Perfect!" Mrs. Funderbunk said with a smile. She inspected Sophie from head to toe. "Just puff your chest out one tiny bit."

"Can I breathe?" Sophie asked. She looked like she had

been frozen by a magic spell while doing the funky chicken dance.

"It would be better if you didn't," Mrs. Funderbunk said.

Ms. Pierre looked at me like she wished I wasn't breathing, either. And not just temporarily.

Everyone backed away as Sophie stood there, trying to hold the ridiculous posture.

"Is Calvin even here yet?" I asked.

"Shortly, dear," Mrs. Funderbunk said. "Now, stand next to her. You don't really have a good side, so just stare straight at the camera."

I think what she meant to say was that both my sides were perfectly good, so it didn't matter which way I presented them.

Miss Honeywell thrust the makeup brush in my face and started dabbing it on my cheeks and nose.

I almost swatted her hands away. It took every ounce of self control not to sneeze all over them.

"I don't want or need makeup," I said, bobbing and weaving each attempt to jab me in the face with the brush.

"Hold still, Austin. We just need to dull that oily skin for the cameras."

"The good news is that the cameras add ten pounds, so you won't look so scrawny," Mr. Muscalini said. "Do we have time for a triple protein shake for Davenport here?"

Ms. Pierre shook her head. She looked at me like she just smelled a fart, which wasn't out of the question inside a middle school, especially ours.

"Do we really have to do this? I hate Calvin," I said.

Sophie was still mad about the secret admirer, so all she had to do was give me the death stare and I changed my mind.

"Okay. Where do I stand? I can't wait to see Calvin again.

It's been too long." I didn't want any part of Calvin Conklin. The guy was an idiot and always botched my interviews.

Sophie gave me another death stare. It was seemingly the only thing she could do while holding the ridiculous posture.

"What? Too much?" I asked.

5

Sophie and I stood next to Calvin Conklin in front of a camera crew. He wore a crisp suit and his hair was perfectly coiffed. He always looked good, but that was about all he had going for him, in case you haven't heard me talk about him before.

He looked into the TV camera and raised an eyebrow. "Calvin Conklin here from Channel 2 News. I'm standing here inside Cherry Avenue Middle School. I haven't been here since the Gophers got crushed by Riverside after Grimmwolf the Gopher died a horrible death and ruined the football season. Anyhoo, we're here to interview the winner of Channel 2's W.S.T.I.N.K. and 102.3's Cupid's Cutest Couple Host Contest."

I glanced over at Sophie. She was more relaxed than the funky chicken statue that Mrs. Funderbunk had her in before, but she was a little more nervous than I thought she would be. She was normally cool under pressure. Like the coolest.

Calvin continued, "We're here with Sophie Rodriguez and her boyfriend, who shall remain nameless because I do not remember his name. This happy couple won the call-in contest. How does it feel?" Calvin moved the mic over to Sophie.

Sophie spoke really fast. "I'm just so excited to have won the Cupid's Cutest Couple Contest. My boyfriend and I are really going to enjoy the concert, and the limo. And the dinner. Even though he calls it Le Fart."

"I thought it was funny," I said, shrugging.

"Oh, wait just one second," Calvin said, holding his earpiece and concentrating. "You didn't win that contest. You won the party that hosts the contest."

"What do you mean?" Sophie asked, confused.

"What do I mean?" Calvin asked. He held his earpiece and said, "No, really. What do I mean, Ted?" After a few seconds, he looked back at the camera and continued, "I just had a little chat with my imaginary friend. Okay, Ted. Fine. You're my real friend. And he told me that you and four other couples will compete to win those fabulous prizes and to be named Cupid's Cutest Couple."

"Oh," Sophie said, deflated.

And I was flat out ready to run. There was no way I wanted to compete in a couple's competition. It was going to be so embarrassing. And that was before I knew Calvin would be the host of the contest.

Calvin continued, "The good news is that you'll get to see me dressed as Cupid. That's worth more than all the other prizes combined!"

Uh, yeah right.

"Who decides what couples will compete?" Sophie asked.

"The school, along with our promotions team. We're looking for hair-pulling drama and maybe a Camel Clutch. You remember that putz who got put in the Clutch after the science fair?"

He was talking about me. Thankfully, he didn't remember me. I said, "No. Never happened."

"Oh, it certainly happened. And it was fantastic. That Amanda Gluskin really cleaned his clock. Can we play back that video, Ted? No? Aww, come on! Please?" Calvin shook his head and looked back at the camera. "Ted says no. Sometimes, he's just no fun. I'll post it on all my social media pages, though, so everyone can enjoy!"

Oh, great. Thanks for that, Calvin.

Calvin continued, "Well, thanks for tuning in. I'm sure

you didn't really care all that much about what I said. Polling shows that you just like to see my face. My grandmother always used to tell me it would be my moneymaker. And my butt, too. But that was kinda weird. Back to you, Ted." Calvin held his earpiece and asked, "You guys want me to turn around so you can get a shot of my butt? No? You sure? You gotta give the audience what they want, no? They don't want to see my butt? That's embarrassing."

Sophie and I just looked at each other, as Calvin rushed toward the camera on the verge of tears. He pushed the camera away. "I'm hideous!" He ran from the Atrium.

Nobody said a word until the doors slammed behind him.

Sophie was stunned. "What just happened?"

"I don't know. You didn't realize that was the deal?"

"No, I guess I just got caught up in winning cutest couple with you that I didn't realized there was more to it." Sophie took a deep breath and said, "Well, we'll just have to win it all. I mean, who's cuter than us?"

"There's nobody cuter. My mother told me, so it must be true."

What had I done? I was doomed.

6

Sophie and I were both early to science class. There was still a little bit of tension. Mr. Gifford strolled over, which was a welcomed move that would certainly break up the uncomfortable silence.

"I heard about the big contest," Mr. Gifford said, stopping at our lab table. "Pretty cool how you guys won the contest, Cutest Couple."

"Well, we won the party," Sophie said. "We still have to win the contest."

"Huh?" Mr. Gifford said, scratching his head.

"It's complicated," I said. "Don't worry about it."

"I think I want to take someone to the dance," Mr. Gifford said.

"Do teachers bring dates to student dances?" I asked.

"Good point," Mr. Gifford said, thinking. "What if I ask a teacher who will double as a chaperone?"

"Who would you ask?" Sophie questioned.

"Mrs. Funderbunk is kind of cute."

Sophie and I both looked at each other.

"She's a little bit full of herself," Sophie said.

"Madeline? No," Mr. Gifford scoffed.

"She only refers to herself in the third person," I said.

"That's what theatre people do, don't they?"

I didn't have a lot of theatre people experience to go on, but I didn't think so.

"Well, I'm going to ask her."

"Ok. Good luck," I said.

"Will you be there for moral support?"

"Umm, I guess so," I said. It was weird, but it fit with Mr. Gifford and his love life. It would not be the first time I would help him out of a love jam.

~

AFTER SCIENCE, I walked with Sophie down the hall to our next classes. My Spidey senses started tingling, as I noticed the waves of students ahead of us were parting like Moses parted the Red Sea. It was an early warning sign that something or someone that you didn't want to be around, was heading your way.

And sure enough, as the pack in front of us parted, that someone was revealed to us as Regan Storm, the evil and obnoxious on-and-off again girlfriend of Randy Warblemacher, of similar evil and obnoxiousness.

Due to my great luck, she was heading straight toward us.

Regan smiled. Don't let that fool you. "Congrats on winning the party," she said, cheerily. Again, don't get sucked in...

"Thanks," Sophie said, as we continued to walk.

Regan stepped in front of Sophie. We both stopped. See what I mean?

"As you know, Randy and I are the IT couple at this

school, so it's only fitting that we win Cupid's Cutest Couple Contest. Enjoy the party, because you're not going to win the contest." Regan smiled as if she hadn't just punched Sophie in the gut with her words.

"We'll see about that, won't we?" Sophie said.

"We won't," Regan said, walking away. "We've already won it."

Sophie stared at Regan as she walked away.

It was just what I needed. A contest with Randy and Regan. True, the last one worked out, but still, they were horrible people who lived to embarrass me and cheated like crazy.

∼

LATER THAT NIGHT, I sat at the dinner table with the whole

family, which didn't happen often those days. With every-one's sports (not mine), clubs, and my parents' work sched-ules, we were always on the run.

My parents always liked to talk at dinner. It was annoy-ing, but what can you do? They put the roof over our heads and food on our plates.

My mom asked, "So, what's going on at school?"

Nobody answered. I hoped Leighton would say some-thing. I knew for certain that Derek wouldn't offer any info.

My mom said, "Anybody?"

I finished chewing my food and said, "Everybody's crazy about the whole Cupid Contest. We got interviewed by Calvin Conklin."

"I'll be sure to check that out," Derek said. "I'm sure you embarrassed yourself yet again."

"Derek, be nice," my father said.

"It wasn't that bad," I said.

"I asked Mia Graves out," Derek said.

"What did she say?" Leighton asked.

"Yes, of course," Derek said, like it was the dumbest question ever asked in the history of questions.

"Oh, right, because no girl could ever say no to you. Didn't Sophie reject Derek?" Leighton asked, looking at me.

"That was one of the best days of my life," I said.

"Kids, come on. Knock it off," my dad said.

"Seriously, though. You must really like her with Valen-tine's Day coming up. In high school, the boys are breaking up with girls left and right, hiding under desks and in lock-ers, trying to avoid all the girls."

"Ah, shoot," Derek said, smacking himself in the fore-head. I thought about punching him in his butt chin, but then thought better of it. Derek continued, "Should I break up with her and then ask her back out on the 15th? Am I gonna have to shell out a whole wad of cash?"

"Instead of being a jerk, why not buy her a rose and take her to the dance," Leighton said.

"The roses at school are like $5!"

"You're a real romantic," my mom said. She looked at my father. "You need to fix that."

"This Mia sounds like a lucky girl," I said, sarcastically. I had just dropped $50 on the robo dialer for Sophie and he was complaining about $5? Without his butt chin, he would be doomed.

Derek looked at my father. "Dad, can I have $5?"

"Clean your room," he said, simply.

"I did."

"This year."

"It's only January."

"This decade then."

"Can we change the subject?" Derek asked. "Austin is gonna have to compete in the Cupid Contest. I can't wait to watch that."

"I thought you won?" my dad asked.

"Long story," I said, with a sigh. We still have to compete to see who wins the whole thing. We just won the pleasure of having Calvin embarrass us."

"Sounds like you're really enthused," my mom said, laughing.

"I don't want to embarrass myself in front of the whole school. And Sophie."

"You've never had a problem embarrassing yourself before," Derek said.

"True, but I usually don't know that I'm going to embarrass myself before it happens."

"Oh, really? Everybody else knows it's gonna happen," Derek said, nonchalantly.

"Derek, come on," my dad said.

"Maybe you should practice," Derek said.

"Embarrassing myself?"

"No, for the contest."

It was one of his better ideas, but how do you practice for a love contest?

7

Love was in the air. In the Atrium. As I walked into school with Ben and Sammie the next morning, there was a Valentine's Day fundraiser going on. Mrs. Trugman was seemingly taking full advantage of the contest. The PTA was selling roses and chocolate, and urging kids to secure their tickets and dates to the dance.

Thankfully, my date was fully secure without having to spend the twelve bucks for the rose and chocolate combo. I hate to admit it, but I kind of agreed with Derek.

Just Charles and Luke were chilling on a bench, talking. Cheryl Van Snoogle-Something was standing with Ditzy Dayna and Brad Melon, who was basically the dude version of Ditzy Dayna. I wasn't sure if Just Charles and Cheryl hadn't seen each other or if she was still mad at him about forgetting the dance.

"Hey, guys," I said, as we approached.

"Dudes," Luke said, and then looked at Sammie, "Dudette."

Just Charles just nodded.

"Cheryl's over there," I said, nodding my head in her direction.

"Oh, yeah?" Just Charles perked up. He looked over to Cheryl and stood up. "I should go talk to her."

Luke looked over and said, "Hey, look at Lincoln Madison. He's got a rose and candy. Who's he gonna ask out? Any bets on whether or not he gets rejected?"

"Poor guy," Ben said. "Just a slave to the corporate system."

"Wait," Just Charles said, nervously. "I think he's going..."

"To ask Cheryl," I said, finishing his sentence. We were all in shock.

Lincoln approached with a smile. We couldn't see Cheryl's reaction as her back was to us, but she took the candy and rose from him.

"You should go over there, dude."

He looked at me. "Come with me."

"I don't want to come with you."

"Please?"

"Fine," I said, following his lead, as he walked toward Cheryl, who continued to talk to Lincoln as we approached.

"Hey!" Just Charles said, overly excited to see everyone. He was forcing it just a little bit too much.

Cheryl turned around as Lincoln scurried away.

"Hey," Cheryl said, less than enthused.

"Whatcha got there," Just Charles asked, his voice shaking.

"Lincoln just asked me to the dance."

Just Charles nodded, seemingly not sure what to say, or trying to hold the tears in.

"What did you say?" I asked.

"I told him I was already going with Just Charles."

"What? How could- oh, wait. That's me," Just Charles said. He broke out into a huge smile, but then it quickly turned into a frown. "Why'd you keep the rose and chocolate?"

Cheryl shrugged. "I didn't want to make him feel bad."

"What are you gonna do with it?"

"I don't know. Eat the chocolate and put the rose in a vase? Normal stuff."

"Oh," Just Charles said, disappointed.

"Or I'll just give it away," Cheryl said. "It's not a big deal."

"I'll eat it," Brad said.

Cheryl shrugged. "Okay." She handed Brad the chocolate and the rose.

Brad grabbed them both, looked at the petals on the rose and bit the entire flower off the stem in one bite. He chewed it as we all stared in shock.

With his mouth full of petals, Brad said, "This is tasty."

Ditzy Dayna looked at me and said, "Brad asked me to the dance. He wants to compete in the contest, too."

"Fantastic," I said. I wasn't overly concerned about the competition. Do I really need to explain why?

"I've always just wanted that Romeo and Juliet love story," Dayna said.

"Really? Why? They knew each other for a day, got married, and ended up dead within a week. And he was dating her cousin right before that."

"Really? What a jerk."

The warning bell rang. It was time to head off to Advisory. I walked with Just Charles and Luke down the hall.

"That wasn't good," Just Charles said.

"What? The whole thing when your girlfriend wanted to keep flowers from another dude?" Luke said, unhelpfully.

"Yeah, I think I really messed up." Just Charles looked at

me and asked, "Can you talk to Lincoln? Maybe get him to back off?"

"I'll try," I said. I was fast becoming the relationship guru of Cherry Avenue. I could barely keep myself from getting dumped half the time. Not sure why everyone trusted me so much with their hearts.

~

I CAUGHT up with Lincoln before English class. I slid into the desk next to him while we waited for the bell. Lincoln was drawing hearts on his notebook with the initials, "L.M." and "C.V.S.S." inside a giant heart.

"Hey, dude. What's going on with Cheryl? You know she's with Just Charles, right?" I said.

"I don't have anything against him, but I think I love her."

I did my best impression of my mother talking to Leighton about all the dumb boys she supposedly loved. "You don't know what love is. You're still so young. You have your whole life ahead of you." I didn't really know what it all meant, but it sounded good.

"I've never felt this way my whole life."

"You're only twelve."

"She's so smart. And fearless. Did you read her news story about the time she went undercover to figure out what was in the school's seafood surprise? She's amazing. I want to be Lincoln Van Snoogle-Something! I'm not afraid to say it."

"You should be, dude. That's weird."

"I'm going for it. Nobody's gonna stop me. Not you. Not Charles. Not the insane $12 I just spent on chocolate and a rose. Nothing."

"What about Amanda Gluskin?" I asked.

"I want to grow old with Cheryl, dude. Not smashed into a thousand pieces for looking at Amanda wrong."

"Good point. Just a thought."

Thankfully, the bell rang. It was English class, so we definitely could've just continued our conversation, as Mrs. Conklin didn't care if the place was on fire, she got her lesson plan done. We could've probably screamed our conversation and have been okay. Maybe we would've been embarrassed in front of our peers, but we wouldn't have gotten in trouble.

~

AFTER CLASS, I took the east wing stairs. I knew that Just Charles, Sammie, and Ben typically met up there for a few minutes before they had science.

I was still about ten steps from them, when Just Charles yelled out, "What did he say?"

"You've got competition, bro. He's not gonna back down. He says he's in love. He wants to take her last name. Maybe you should beat him to the punch," I said, stopping in front of them.

'Just Charles Herbert Zaino-Van Snoogle-Something..." Just Charles said, thinking aloud. "I like the sound of it."

"Oh, God. I was kidding," I said.

"It's my first Valentine's Day that I won't be soul-crushingly alone. I can't lose her now!"

"Dude, you're twelve!" Ben said.

"Thank you," I said to Ben.

"I'm going to smile at Allie today."

I couldn't help but laugh. "We've got two kids looking to

marry Cheryl and you're ready to smile at a girl? This is all too much."

"You're really moving at a blistering pace," Just Charles said.

Sammie added, "Yeah, at that pace you're more likely to ask her to the high school prom than this dance."

"Zip it. I know what I'm doing."

I looked at Ben. He didn't seem to have too much confidence in that answer.

He read my mind and said, "I'm playing the long game."

"Maybe you guys will get together when you end up at Vintage Retirement Community. You can look for your dentures together," I said.

"Funny. Not."

Sammie looked at me and asked, "You talk to Randy yet?"

"No, and I don't plan to. Sophie and I had a little run-in with Regan."

"He's telling everyone he's gonna crush you in the contest and win the whole thing."

"Oh, really? What else did he say?"

"That you were short, stupid, annoying."

"Ok, that's enough," I said.

Sammie continued, counting on her fingers, "Didn't know why Sophie was dating you. You slurp your soup disgustingly."

"I don't even eat soup!"

"So, you agree with the rest of them?" Ben asked.

"No! Well, half of them. I'm short and not sure why Sophie is dating me, either."

"Randy," Just Charles said. He didn't have to say anything else. We all knew what he meant. Just for the record, if anyone just says, "Randy," you can immediately add "is an idiot."

I shook my head. "I don't know how many times I can crush him and he just keeps coming at me. Maybe I should just let him win and he'll get bored with me." I thought for a minute. "Nah, I want to crush him."

As I headed to my next class, everyone seemed excited about the contest, except for me, that is.

Jimmy Trugman asked, "You ready for the contest?"

I shrugged.

"I hope you win, bro."

Pamela Wentz said, "Great job on winning the dance. I love DJ Fight Club!"

I gave her a thumbs up.

Randy Warblemacher said, "I'm gonna crush your stupid face! This is gonna be fun."

"Looking forward to it," I said.

~

BEFORE THE BELL rang to end another glorious day at Cherry Avenue Middle School, the Speaker of Doom crackled.

Ms. Pierre's voice boomed into our classroom. "Please note that anyone who wishes to participate in the Cupid's Cutest Couple Contest should submit their applications and essay by fifth period in the main office tomorrow. Said applications will not be available until after first period. Also, the main office will not be accepting applications during third and fourth period."

Gavin Ross said, "When the heck are we supposed to sign up? Or write an essay?"

I was already in the contest, so I didn't care all that much about it.

"It doesn't matter, anyway," a voice next to me said.

A normally-quiet girl, Emily Springer sat next to me, doodling.

"What doesn't?" I asked.

"Randy and Regan are gonna win the whole thing."

"We'll see about that," I said.

I looked over to see Emily's drawing on her notebook. There was a heart and in script, it read, 'I love R.W.' and 'E.S. & R.W. 4-Eva'

"What do you actually see in Randy?" I asked, annoyed.

She didn't look up, but answered my question. "He's so dreamy. Those eyes. He's smart. And so courageous. I love watching him play football."

"Okay, that's enough." I thought I might puke.

But Emily continued, "Did I say handsome? His hair. I just want to run my fingers through it all day and then smell them."

"That's really weird," I said.

In her defense, the whole place was weird and it was getting worse as Valentine's Day approached.

8

Ben had promised he was going to make contact with Allie before lunch. He was so nervous, I had to remind him that she was just a girl and that he was not attempting to make contact with some sort of alien being from another planet, although sometimes girls do seem that way to me.

So, I was holding my breath, sitting with Sophie and Sammie in the cafeteria as the bell rang. Ben was nowhere to be found. Had he been annihilated by a hostile alien simply for a smile? Or maybe he was so bold as to include a wink?

I exhaled as Ben entered the cafeteria all smiles. He survived the alien encounter and lived to tell the tale!

"How'd it go?" I called to him as he approached.

"Huge success!" Ben said with a fist pump.

"Great! Tell us about it."

Ben slipped into the seat next to Sammie across from Sophie and me. He said, "I smiled at her. She smiled back."

"That's it?" Sammie asked.

"Yeah, that was the plan, right?"

"It was," I said. But after hearing about it then, I think we all thought it could've been a little more aggressive.

"Did you wait for her to say hi?" Sammie asked.

"Yeah, that didn't go as well," he said, his voice trailing off.

"What happened?" Sophie asked.

"You know how I used to go penguin when I got really nervous?"

"Oh, God," I said.

When Ben tried out for the school musical, his body froze and he waddled out onto the stage like a penguin. Ben continued, "Well, I kinda went caveman."

"What does that mean?" Sammie asked.

"Well, she walked over toward me. I pretended to tie my shoe. I timed it perfectly and stood up right as she was a few feet away from me. I said, 'Hi.' She said, 'Hi.'"

"So, that's what we planned, right?" I asked.

"Yeah, but then she said, 'You're Ben, right?' and I said, 'Yes, me Ben.'"

"Oooh," Sammie said.

"Maybe she didn't pick up on it." Sophie said.

Ben shrugged. "I felt like I should swing on a vine out of the room like Tarzan or something."

"What did she do?" I asked.

"She kind of just giggled."

"That's good," Sophie said.

"Giggling is good? I wasn't trying to be funny."

I asked, "Was it laughter with pointing? I get that a lot."

"No, it was girlie giggling," Sammie said, and rubbed his shoulder. "It's okay."

"I think it was great, Ben!" Sophie said.

"That was a power move, Benny! A. Power. Move," I said. I was making a bigger deal out of it than it truly was, but he needed the confidence.

I swung my hand toward him for a high five, but he was

late. Our hands missed and I ended up slapping and squashing the corned beef casserole on my tray. I must admit, it looked better after I hit it.

As I wiped my hand with a napkin, Katrina Quinn came over with a smile.

"Hey, Austin," she said, shyly.

"Oh, hi, Katrina. What's up?"

She twirled her hair as she spoke. "Just thought you should know that I was in the main office last period and they were out of applications for the contest. A lot of kids tried to sign up, but couldn't."

"What did they say?" I asked.

"They told everyone they were fresh out. It seemed kinda fishy, so I thought you should know."

"Thanks. I appreciate that."

"Well, bye," Katrina said with a wave and a giggle.

I furrowed my brow as she walked away.

"I think we know who Austin's secret admirer is," Sophie said, less than excited.

"Why do you say that?" I asked. Dumb question, I know.

"The hair twirling. The giggling."

Sammie looked at Ben and said, "See, giggling is a good thing."

"Not for her, it isn't," Sophie said, staring at Katrina across the room.

"Relax," I said. Note to all dudes: don't tell your lady friends to relax. It only amps up their need for more "relaxation", if you know what I mean.

The rest of lunch was on the quiet side. Sophie was less than enthused. I couldn't wait to get out of there. Finally, the bell rang. As we left lunch, Mia Graves rushed over to us.

"Austin!" Mia called.

I knew who she was, but wasn't friends with her at all. I looked over, not sure if she was talking to a different Austin, even though there weren't any others. I mean, how could there be? After I realized she was talking to me, I was afraid that Sophie might clothesline her or something.

"Hi, Mia. What's up?"

"I wanted to tell you that I signed up for the contest with Derek. Isn't that exciting?"

Ugh. "Yeah, totally," I said. I was disgusted. First, Randy (the idiot) and then Derek (the doofus). I was half expecting to find out that our old principal, Prince Butt Hair, would be competing as well.

"You were able to sign up? Everybody's been complaining about it," Sophie said.

"It was easy. Mrs. Murphy had one waiting for me."

I was still speechless. Not only couldn't I believe Derek would be in the competition, but they were seemingly only giving out applications to certain people. And then Derek walked up to us.

"Why are you talking to him?" Derek asked Mia.

"He's your brother. I was just telling him that I signed us up for the contest."

"What contest?" Derek asked like the idiot that he was. Or doofus.

"I told you about it last night, silly," Mia said.

"Oh, yeah. The one where I get to beat Austin? I mean that's pretty much every contest I have with Austin. Count me in."

"Don't you want to win Cutest Couple with me?"

"Oh, yeah. That, too. But the Austin thing is my main motivation."

"Your chivalry is inspiring," I said. "You're every girl's dream."

"I have to set a good example for you," Derek said.

"Right..."

"Later, goofball," Derek said, as he grabbed Mia's hand and changed course.

"Good luck at the contest!" Mia yelled after us.

"Can you believe that?" I asked Sophie. "This is unbelievable."

Sophie and I were cutting through the Atrium, when Luke and Just Charles caught my eye. They headed over to us.

Luke leaned in and whispered, "So, what's the plan?"

"The plan with what?" I asked.

"The dance, dude," Just Charles said.

"To attend," I said.

"What do you mean? That's so boring," Luke said.

"What did you have in mind?" Sophie asked.

Luke was shocked. "Well, we saved one dance, took down another. I figured we would have to raise our game. Dances seem so meaningless when they're not on the verge of collapse."

"Well, I'm gonna compete in the contest," I said. "That'll be good enough for me."

"Yeah, that'll be entertaining," Luke said. "I need something, dude. I've got to impress Allie."

I just stared at him. Most of the time, I wasn't trying to entertain anyone.

"What? Sorry. Not sorry. You're always embarrassing yourself. It's part of your charm."

I shrugged. He was pretty spot on.

"What are you gonna do for the Grand Gesture of Love?" Luke asked, trying not to laugh.

It was a good question. "I'm working on something amazing," I lied.

Sophie's face broke out into a broad smile. "I know it'll be great."

That made one of us. I had no idea what I was going to do.

9

The next morning was a doozy. Like from minute one. As I walked into the Atrium with Ben and Sammie, my eyes were drawn to the enormous sign hanging on the wall and the crowd in front of it. It was a long, white banner that stretched at least eight feet wide. In red, it read, "Austin, Be Mine!"

"What the heck is that?" I said, to no one in particular.

"Whoa, dude," was all Ben could muster.

As we walked closer to the sign, I asked Sammie, "Did Sophie mention anything about this?"

"Nope," she said, shaking her head.

"Well, there she is," Ben said, pointing across the Atrium.

I smiled as Sophie approached. "Thanks, but it's a bit much, no?"

She looked up at it with a frown on her face. "I didn't do that. It must be your secret admirer."

"Don't worry about it. I don't know who it is and I don't care."

"I care," Sophie said, staring at it.

"Can't we just pretend it's from you?" I asked. "Nobody has to know."

"I know." Sophie walked away in a huff.

Ugh. "I didn't do anything wrong," I called out. I looked at Sammie and said, "Can you please talk to her? How can she be mad at me?"

"I will," Sammie said, and headed after Sophie.

I stood there with Ben, stupefied.

After a minute, I said to Ben, "Look, there's Allie. Maybe you should go talk to her."

"She's talking to Gary Kingsley."

"So? What does Gary Kingsley have that you don't?"

"He can fart the alphabet. I can only burp it."

"I'm not sure that's a good thing," I said. "What else?"

"I don't know."

"So, nothing. Go over there and ask her if she's excited to see DJ Fight Club."

"I don't know if I can do that. I'm afraid I'll caveman it again."

"She liked it, so maybe try it again. You could say, 'Me like DJ Fight Club. You like DJ Fight Club?'"

"You're such an idiot," he said. "I'm only doing this to get away from you."

"Good luck, Tarzan."

Ben shook his head as he walked over to Allie. He paced around behind her as she and Gary continued talking.

Then Luke walked up behind me. Sometimes we call him Luke the Lurker. He just slips into the conversation and scares the poop out of everyone. Like at that moment.

"What's up, Butter Cup?" Luke said in my ear.

"Ahhh, farts! Dude, you drive me nuts with that."

"Sorry. Not sorry."

I turned around to look at him. I was immediately taken aback. "What the heck are you wearing?"

As I analyzed his outfit, the problem wasn't necessarily what he was wearing. It was more how he was wearing it. He wore jeans with rips and tears everywhere. It was legit cool. For a shirt, he had a plaid button down. Nice, if not plain. But he had a solid four buttons unbuttoned with nothing underneath it. His chest was bare for everyone to see.

"Chicks love chest hair," Luke said with a smile.

"And?" I asked.

"Allie wants a real man. Well, here I come."

"You don't have chest hair," I said.

"Do, too!"

"The millimeter fuzzy blond stuff doesn't count," I said, pointing to the barely visible peach fuzz on his chest. "Everybody knows that."

"Really? It should totally count," Luke said, disappointed.

"Some babies have more chest hair when they're born than you have right now."

"That hurts. Why do you have to be so mean?" Luke asked. He puffed his chest out. "I'm not gonna let that stop me."

"Where are you going?" I asked.

"I'm going to talk to Allie," Luke said.

He was off before I could stop him. Just as Gary was walking away from Allie, Luke slipped in between her and Ben, boxing him out. His lurking skills were on point. It wasn't as bad as the time he tried to box me out for the spotlight at one of the bar mitzvahs our band played, but it wasn't good, either. And I felt bad for Ben. He had worked up his courage and he was thwarted. By a good friend, no less.

As I was watching Ben continue to pace around the Atrium, Zorch strolled up to me. He was an all-around good dude. He'd helped me out of more jams than I could count and let me get away with a whole lot of stuff that most people wouldn't.

"Nice sign," he said. "Sophie's a sweetheart."

"She didn't do it. I'm guessing you don't know who did it, either."

"Oh, no. I just assumed..."

"Me, too. And the crazy thing is, Sophie's mad at me for it. I didn't do it. I don't even want a secret admirer."

"Well, it's always nice to be in demand," Zorch said, sadly. "At least, I think it's probably nice. See you later, buddy."

Jimmy Trugman came over to me and said, "Dude, somebody told me they saw you kissing someone in the stairwell. I knew it wasn't true, but I thought you should know."

"It's not true, but who said it? And who did I supposedly kiss?"

"That's the thing. Details are fuzzy. You know how things spread. Erin Moore told me. She heard it from someone else."

"This is just great," I said, shaking my head.

∽

THINGS GOT EVEN MORE interesting in Advisory. The Speaker of Doom crackled. I know what you're thinking. Why didn't I just blow the thing up already? And the answer is that I have no idea. I mean, I'm like a genius and I have scientific superpowers. It would've been a cake walk. Anyway...

"Good morning, Gophers," Ms. Pierre said, sweetly. "It's my pleasure to announce the upcoming contestants for Cupid's Cutest Couple Contest."

"Oh, boy," I said to Just Charles next to me. "Here we go."

"Sophie Rodriguez and Austin Davenport," Ms. Pierre said like she was gonna puke. "Kara Wendell and Lionel Lamar."

"Isn't that the surfer dude who thinks he's a life philosopher?" I asked.

"I think so."

"Dayna Jeffries and Brad Melon," Ms. Pierre said.

"Oh, man. Brad Mellon is dumber than Dayna, so there's no way they're winning," Just Charles said.

Ms. Pierre continued, "Mia Graves and Derek Davenport."

"What? This is gonna be the worst." I hung my head in my hands.

And then she dropped the bomb. "And finally, Regan Storm and Randy Warblemacher."

"Why?" I shrieked to the heavens. The entire class stared at me as I banged my head on the desk, repeatedly. It was kind of therapeutic. I think I was in a soothing coma for most of first period. When I woke up, I thought it was all a dream.

I wiped the drool from my face, as Mrs. Callahan was in mid-sentence.

Just Charles looked at me and said, "Dude, you okay?"

"Yeah," I whispered. "I had the worst dream. Both Derek and Randy got into the contest."

"That wasn't a dream, bro."

"What?" I yelled.

"Austin, is everything okay?" Mrs. Callahan said, as the entire class stared at me.

"I'm living a nightmare, but besides that, everything is

fabulous!" I gave her a big thumbs up and forced a smile for good measure.

Once class was over, I walked out of the room with Just Charles.

"I am not happy," I said.

"Oh, that's a surprise. I couldn't tell when you were rocking yourself to sleep. Or into a coma. Or whatever that was."

"I was meditating," I said.

Just Charles wasn't paying attention to me. "Man, I really wanted to get in. They wouldn't even give me a form to fill out. This whole thing is a setup."

I couldn't agree more.

10

As I headed to my next class, I walked past the main office and stopped dead in my tracks. I needed to figure out what the heck was going on with the contest. I opened the door and slipped in. I still had a few minutes to get to class. I walked up to the front desk.

"Excuse me, Mrs. Murphy?"

"Austin? Nobody called you down. You probably want to skedaddle before you get detention."

"Thanks for the heads up, but I'm really trying to figure out what happened with the contest. A lot of people wanted to sign up who didn't get the chance."

"It was chaos. We ran out of forms, so there weren't a lot of sign-ups."

"How do you run out of forms when the copier is right there?"

Ms. Pierre peeked out of her office, which I still affectionately called The Butt Crack, even though it was no longer home to the biggest butt I knew, Principal Buthaire. She stared at me with a furrowed brow.

Mrs. Murphy just shrugged.

"The fix is in," I whispered. "But what else is new at this school?"

I turned and walked out, just shaking my head.

On my way out, I had the pleasure of bumping into Randy. He smiled. I didn't have time for his shenanigans. I rarely ever did, but I was so fuming mad, I wanted nothing to do with him.

I stepped around him, but he stepped in front of me.

"Well, an interesting bunch has been assembled for the contest, hasn't it?" He didn't wait for an answer. "This is my official 'I'm going to crush you' warning. You have been served, Davenfart."

I didn't have anything to say. Randy turned to walk away, but turned back.

"It's funny, Davenfart. I used to think you were dumb, but I truly believe that you enjoy being a loser."

"Just get your insults out and move on, please."

"I have a pretty long list. I've been writing them down as they pop into my head."

"Do you want to just text them to me?" I asked.

"I don't have your phone number. I don't even want your phone number. Oh, I should add that to my insult list."

"You're such an idiot." My own list of Randy insults was growing by the second.

～

I STOOD with Ben and Sammie at my locker, about to head to the cafeteria, when Luke the Lurker slid in next to Ben and scared the farts out of us again.

"What's up, kids?" he said.

"You're rather cheerful," Sammie said.

"Yep. I asked Allie to the dance."

"What did she say?" Ben asked, nervously.

"She said she was keeping her options open, but there was still time to impress her."

"Ooh, that's tough, bro," I said, shutting my locker.

"She didn't say no," Luke said, as we headed toward the cafeteria. Shepherd's pie was on the menu. I hoped it wasn't actual shepherds.

"She didn't say yes," Ben countered. "Keeping her options open means that she's hoping someone better asks."

"Someone better? I don't think that's possible," Luke scoffed.

"I don't think you've looked in the mirror lately," I said.

"Very funny. Who's better than me?"

Sammie looked around the hallway and started pointing. "That guy and that guy and that guy."

Luke said, "Okay. Enough."

Sammie continued, "And that guy. And this guy." She was pointing to Ben.

"Ben? Oh, is that so?" Luke asked, chuckling. "You're gonna ask her to the dance?"

"Yes," Ben said.

I was surprised, but then again, he didn't say which dance he would invite her to. He could've been thinking about the Vintage Retirement Community Prom.

"I'd like to see you try," Luke said. "Go do it now."

"I'm not gonna do it now. I need to plan my approach."

"What are you, chicken?"

I scratched my head and asked, "Why are you trying to get him to ask her if you want her to go with you?"

"Oh, yeah. Good point," Luke said. "You should go with Sammie. Weren't you guys gonna go to the Halloween dance together before we got banned?"

"That was an unconfirmed rumor," Ben said.

I looked over at Sammie, who was fidgeting with her pocketbook and looking down at her shoes.

We were almost at lunch when I heard Mr. Gifford call out to me, "Austin! Over here. Need your romantic advice. I mean, I have a homework question for you."

I looked at my crew and said, "I'll meet you over there. Don't eat all the sheperd's pie without me."

Mr. Gifford slid in beside me. "Mrs. Funderbunk stands outside the music room before the bell rings. I'm gonna ask her right now."

"Okay. Good luck."

"I need you there. Just hang close. I think I've got it, but if you need to join in, feel free."

"Join in?" What the heck was going on? I was not qualified to 'join in' to the romantic relationships of teachers. Or any adult for that matter.

"Yeah, in case I crash and burn," he said, like it was a usual occurrence. He pointed down the hallway. "There she is. My love."

I just shook my head and slipped into the closest herd of sixth graders, which was within ear shot of where Mrs. Funderbunk stood.

"Madeline, my dear," Mr. Gifford said. "How are you?" He grabbed her hand and kissed it.

"Madeline is doing well. And you?"

"Fine. Fine," Mr. Gifford said.

"To what does Mrs. Funderbunk owe the pleasure of a visit from Cherry Avenue's finest scientist?"

"Oh, you embarrass me. I was wondering if you would do me the honor of accompanying me, as my date, to the school's Valentine's Day dance? DJ Fight Club will be there."

"I have a date with the phantom."

"Who's that?" Mr. Gifford said, confused. "Sounds mysterious."

"The Phantom of the Opera. But even if the phantom was busy, Madeline Funderbunk would probably say no."

"Oh, I see," Mr. Gifford said.

I didn't know what to do. He wanted me to 'join in' if things went poorly, but I had nothing to add.

Mrs. Funderbunk continued, "I'm sorry to hurt your

feelings. But it's not Mrs. Funderbunk. It's you. But the good news is you have a lot of room for improvement."

"Oh, that's okay. I'll just wallow in loneliness and self-pity for all of eternity, but I'll get over it eventually." Mr. Gifford walked away, hanging his head.

I tried to follow Mr. Gifford, but a wave of sixth-graders rushed down the hall, heading for class, before I could catch up to him. I tried to fight the wave, but eventually I just gave in and let it sweep me away.

I barely made it to lunch before the bell rang. Sophie was staring at me, which wasn't a good sign. She did not look happy.

I slipped into the seat next to her. She scooted over a few inches away from me.

"I'm sure you heard the rumor," I said. "I did not kiss anyone in any staircase or anyplace else in this school. I kissed nobody, nowhere." I seriously hoped there wasn't a new girl named Nobody Nowhere. That would be my kind of luck. "Somebody is messing with us."

"It's probably your secret admirer," Sophie spat.

"She's not mine. I don't want any part of her or this," I said.

"Whatever," Sophie said with her no-way-is-this-just-a-whatever-situation tone.

Ugh.

11

I was not at all happy. Somebody was messing with my relationship with Sophie. But who was it? I had no idea. I mean, there were suspects, but no evidence of anything. There was a good chance it was Randy, but it could be a legitimate admirer. If Sophie liked me, so could someone else, right? It could also be Butt Hair's revenge, or even Ms. Pierre? I didn't know why she still hated me. My takedown of Principal Buthaire led to her getting a promotion. I wondered if she was married. Maybe I could set her up with someone, given my extensive relationship experience, so she would get off my case.

All of a sudden, Ms. Pierre appeared out of nowhere. It was like Beetlejuice, only I didn't even have to say her name three times. I just thought about her. Once. She was a scary one.

"Misterrrr Davenport. You're late for fifth period."

I thought for a quick second and said, "But it's sixth period."

"And there you have it. Detention."

"Aww, come on," I muttered.

"Ms. Pierre, are you married?" I asked, while checking her hand for a wedding ring.

"Perhaps," she said. Ms. Pierre ripped off the detention slip and dropped it.

The piece of paper floated down through the air and settled on the floor. I reached down to get the detention slip and looked up in shock as I heard a bang and saw a bright light and smoke.

As much as I hated her, I was impressed. She had just disappeared using a ninja smoke bomb. Principal Buthaire would never have been cool enough to try that.

◦∼◦

SCIENCE WAS A JOY. Mr. Gifford was missing, most likely due to the Mrs. Funderbunk fiasco, so Mr. Muscalini was asked to fill in for our class because he was on a break. And there were still all the rumors about Sophie and me swirling around. And they were getting worse.

Sophie walked in and dropped her books on the table.

"Hey," I said.

"Hey," Sophie said, monotone.

I was just about to tell her that I didn't want to be with anyone but her, when Randy walked in. "Davenfart, did Sophie break up with you yet? Kissing another girl in the stairwell. I can't believe anyone would want to kiss you."

"Shut up, Randy," I said and then to Sophie, "See? Nobody wants to kiss me. Randy says so."

"Randy's a liar. You're always saying that."

"Not always," I said, defeated.

Thankfully, Mr. Muscalini entered the classroom and

said, "Today, we are going to talk about the science of protein shakes."

I needed a break. There was only one place in any public school that I knew of to get a break. And that was Max's Comfort Station. Max was basically the Wizard of Oz, but with potties. And then some.

I just got up and walked out of the room.

Randy called after me, "Don't kiss anyone in the hallway."

Idiot.

I headed down the stairs (and didn't kiss anyone) and down the hall into the east wing. I opened the door and walked in. Normally, it was pretty quiet. That day, it was anything but. I nearly hit Chase Marin with the door and there were a solid six people in front of him. Max had even increased his staff. Typically, he was a sole proprietor. He had an assistant, who seemed to be gathering Valentine's Day items for Max's customers.

There were flowers, chocolates, greeting cards, and teddy bears organized around the bathroom.

"What the heck is going on here?" I said to no one in particular.

Max called out to everyone, "Sorry about the wait, everyone. This is our busiest time of the year."

I didn't realize there was a busy time for peeing.

Chase asked, "Are you still offering the matchmaking, match breaking services?"

"I'm not breaking anybody up these days. Bad karma, bro. If you want an introduction to a girl you have your eye on, I can take care of that for you. It's $10. $20 if she's a cheerleader or a grade ahead of you. And of course, we have all of the special additions to make your significant other feel special. Our teddy bear and rose combination is a particularly good deal and always well received."

Two eighth-grade dudes walked past me and scooted out the door, barely able to carry all of the romantic goods they bought. I kinda knew how Ben felt. It was a big scam. To show your love, you had to buy a whole bunch of stuff that would eventually be tossed aside.

"Aus the Boss! How goes it, bro?" Max said to me, peeking around the line.

"Good. Well, not really, but whatever."

"I know you don't need any matchmaking services, or do you?"

"No. I'm good there. Maybe counseling."

"Ha. I'm sure it's not that bad. Probably nothing that some gourmet chocolates can't fix? Maybe a rose for Ms. Rodriguez?"

"I don't have any money on me. Next time, bro. I didn't realize you offered all of this. I just need a few minutes to chill."

"Whatever you need."

Timmy Haynes, who was a few kids in front of me, asked, "Somebody said something about coaching?"

"Yep," Max said. He pointed to a partition behind him. "On the other side of that wall is our in-house relationship coach. We have one-on-one coaching sessions for you to practice your lines."

"Lines for what? The Shakespeare play?" Another dude asked.

"No, for getting a date to the dance. Sounds like you might need it, if you haven't been practicing."

"Whoa," I said. "People pay for that?"

"Heck yeah," Max said. "The coach is booked all week."

"It's not Mr. Muscalini, is it?"

"No, not that kind of coach," Max laughed. "He would just have 'em run the 44 Blast and run the chicks over. We've got more finesse than that. And there are group sessions, too."

Things were getting serious around Cherry Avenue Middle School.

12

As I walked into school the next day, I thought it would be a normal day. I'm not sure why. It was anything but. There was a whole lot more than love in the air. There was a haze of cologne and perfume stretching across the entire Atrium. I waded through it with Ben and Sammie, covering my nose and mouth, but still coughing.

"It's worse than a stink bomb," Ben said.

"It's not that bad," I said.

"I think I see Allie. Or is that Zorch? I need help," Ben said.

The fumes must've been getting to his head or they were just that thick, because Allie looked nothing like Zorch.

"Just keep pushing, bro."

Eventually, we made it through the fumes and found clean air. We stood next to the open doors that seemed to be feeding the Atrium with fresh oxygen.

"That is Allie," Ben said. "Should I talk to her? What should I say?"

"Yes, and just be yourself," Sammie said.

"Have you seen me?"

"Yes. You're great. I think you just need to be a little more outgoing. A little more confident. We can dress you up a little bit, too."

"Ripped jeans, faux hawk?"

"We'll be calling her Mrs. Gordon before you know it," I said, laughing.

"Hey! I'm not looking for marriage here."

"Maybe we should get you an earring and a chain that attaches to a nose ring. That would be sweet," Sammie said.

"Are you trying to sabotage me?" Ben asked. "Seriously, I don't know what to say."

"Ask her something, like how does it feel without the braces?" I said.

Sammie added, "What does she like to do when she's

not in school? Does she like to dance? And then you can roll into the dance question."

"What dance question?" Ben asked.

"The 'will she go to the dance with you' question," I said. Face palm.

"Oh, right. Maybe you can help me? Whisper stuff to me or help me somehow."

"Okay." I was also thinking of referring him to Max's coach. I wondered if Max would give me a referral fee. Being the leader of Nerd Nation could finally pay off. I had literally a whole nation of dorks who needed massive relationship help.

"Good. We'll talk more in lunch or on the bus later. Gotta go."

"Later, Ben," I said.

"I'll go with you," Sammie said to Ben.

I turned around and nearly bumped into Zorch, confirming that he and Allie were not the same person.

"Hey, buddy," Zorch said, monotone.

"What's the matter, Zorch?" I asked.

"Nothing."

"You seem sad."

"I'm fine."

"No, really. What's the matter?"

"I don't know. I guess I get a little lonely this time of year. Ever since Mrs. Zorch and I got divorced."

That was above my pay grade. "I'm sorry. Well, it's Meatloaf Day. I know you love Miss Geller's meatloaf."

"Yes, I do," Zorch said, a little perkier than before.

"And she's nice," I added.

"She is."

"And pretty."

"Very."

"Well, have a great day."

"I think I will," Zorch said, smiling.

I watched Zorch as I walked away. He had a little more bounce in his step than usual. Meatloaf Day seemed to do the trick. Or was there more to it? Personally, I hated Meatloaf Day. It was more like Deathloaf Day. It actually tasted worse than that. I know it doesn't seem possible, but you haven't had the displeasure of tasting it.

Later, during lunch, a plan started to hatch in my mind as I waited on the hot lunch line and caught Miss Geller's eye.

"Austin, are you waiting for the meatloaf?" she asked, surprised.

"No," I said. I wanted to scream, "Never, you crazy woman!" but I was able to control myself. "But, you know who told me that he loves your meatloaf?"

"Who?" Miss Geller asked, excitedly. I assumed she didn't hear that too often. Or ever.

"Zorch. Mr. Zorch. Eugene. Do you want me to bring him some from you? I'm sure he would really appreciate that."

"Oh, I don't know." She started to blush. "Austin, you're so sweet. How come no meatloaf for you?"

I had to think fast. "Umm. Oh, I'm just looking for something a little lighter."

"Why not have both? I can slop a little extra on there for you," Miss Geller said, with a smile.

"No. I couldn't. I don't want you to run out. I mean, what would everyone do without it?"

"We never run out of the meatloaf," she said, sadly. "I always got the sense nobody liked it."

"No, that's just...poo," I said. Like the meatloaf. "It's really, really, umm, meaty. And totally loafy. I mean, you shape that thing like you went to loafing school or something." Thankfully, my brain told me to stop talking before I sounded like an even bigger idiot than I already did.

"Thanks!" Miss Geller said, cheerily. "I'll pack some up for Mr. Zorch. Pick it up on the way to your next class?"

"Okay."

"You sure you don't want a little slop of loaf?"

"I'm good. Really," I said, forcing a smile through a growing desire to puke.

I slid my tray down the line. I couldn't bare to look at the meat loaf as I passed by. I had a rule. I didn't eat anything that was slopped onto my plate. Pigs ate slop. I was a sophisticated adolescent boy. Ok, so I was pretty much a pig, but still I was a pig with standards.

After I ate, I made the dreaded walk back to the hot lunch line. Going through once was bad enough. I kept telling myself it was for Zorch. It only helped a little. I wretched a few times as the image of a graying loaf of meat kept popping into my head.

Miss Geller saw me and headed my way. She smiled as she handed me a container wrapped in foil.

"Thanks," I said, breathing through my mouth to avoid overloading my senses.

"Give Mr. Zorch my best," she said.

"I will." I hoped she wasn't talking about the meatloaf.

As I walked back to meet Sophie, Ben, and Sammie, I held the loathsome loaf as far away from me as possible. I didn't want the fumes seeping into my clothes or my nose. It was the kind of stench that could make you puke. Just thinking about it almost made me puke.

"Oh, my God. That's disgusting," Sophie said.

Sammie held her nose and said in a nasally voice, "It looks like it has green fumes coming out from it."

"Sorry. She didn't give me hazmat suits for everyone. I'll catch up with you all later if you want to leave me behind."

"Yeah, definitely," Ben said.

"See you later," Sophie said.

"Adios, muchacho," Sammie said, still holding her nose.

"I'll miss you, too," I said, turning down the hall toward Zorch's lair.

As I made my way there, I tried to keep my mind off the meatloaf, but it was really difficult. Mostly because people were pointing at me, disgusted or running to the nearest garbage pail to puke. Not that it was ever good, but the meatloaf seemed to get even worse just a few short minutes after the bell rang.

The stench was horrendous. I assumed Zorch had his entire nasal system removed in the war or something. I wasn't sure he was ever in a war, but I didn't know how else someone could lose their entire nasal system.

I was going to just chuck the decaying disaster into Zorch's lair and be done with it, his love life no longer my main concern. I just wanted to survive. I hadn't told my parents I loved them that morning. And Sophie was still kinda mad at me. I couldn't go out like that. Thankfully, Zorch exited his lair as I approached.

I tossed it into the air and took three steps back. I almost dove behind a garbage pail, not sure if it would explode like a toxic grenade on impact. Zorch caught it, explosion-free.

"Is this what I think it is?" he asked, excitedly. He didn't even wait for an answer. He took a deep whiff of the foil and smiled. "Ahhh, yes. It is. Thank you, Austin."

"You owe me, big time."

"I kinda remember helping you out of more than a few jams."

"Okay. We're even then. This was a big one. I almost died."

Zorch laughed. "Thanks for risking your life for me."

"Forget about it," I said. "Miss Geller was really excited to know that you loved her meatloaf."

"You told her?" Zorch asked, shocked.

"Yeah. This is from her. I think she likes you. You should ask her out."

"Oh, I don't know, Austin."

"Would you rather stay lonely?"

"But what if she says no?"

"Then nothing changes. And maybe you won't like her meatloaf anymore. And that wouldn't be such a bad thing."

13

I sat with Ben, as usual, on the bus for the ride home. Sammie was at cheerleading practice. Ben was still on edge about asking Allie to the dance. He had no idea what to say.

"I told you," I said. "I'll talk you through it."

"How are we gonna do it?" Ben asked.

"You have wireless earbuds, right?"

"Yeah. Why?"

"Wear one. We'll be connected through the phone. You'll call me before you walk over there. I'll talk to you while you talk to her."

"Okay. I feel good about this. Just don't talk in cave man."

"I typically don't. I might talk in Yoda, though."

"Dude! Don't do that to me. I'll probably just repeat everything you say."

"Stop me, you can't," I said with my best Yoda voice.

"Please, don't. I'm begging you," Ben said.

"Dance with me, will you? Smoochie smoochie you, can I?"

~

THE NEXT MORNING, it was go time. I pumped Ben up the entire ride to school and he was ready to make his approach. I stood in front of him in the Atrium with Sammie next to me.

"You ready?" I asked.

"Nope," Ben said. "I'm out."

Sammie grabbed Ben's arm before he could disappear into the crowd, perhaps forever.

"You're amazing," Sammie said. "If she says no, it's her own stupidity."

"Are you saying she's stupid?" Ben asked, defensively.

"No, well, yes, but only if she says no."

"I'm confused."

"Good," I said. "Time to go. Put the ear bud in."

Ben put in his ear bud. Sammie messed with his hair the best she could to try to hide it. I didn't think it was that big of a deal. Most people who had them just walked around with them in, no questions asked. He took out his phone and dialed mine.

I put the phone to my ear. "Master Yoda, this is. Jedi Master and matchmaker, I am."

"Dude, come on," Ben whined. "This is important to me."

"Sorry, I am," I said.

Sammie smacked me.

"Okay. I'm back," I said. "This is a lot less fun, but I've got you covered, bro. Go get 'em, Padawan."

"Wish me luck," Ben said. He took a deep breath and headed across the Atrium toward Allie and her friends.

"He's got a cute walk," Sammie said, mindlessly.

"He walks regular like everyone else."

"No, he has a little bounce."

"That's weird."

I slid over to one of the dogwood trees and watched Ben as he approached Allie.

"She's separating from her pack, which is a good sign," I said.

"What do I say?" Ben whispered.

"Wait until you actually get to her," I said into the phone.

"That's a terrible line. Even I know that."

"I wasn't...Ugh. Just say, 'Hey' and see what she says." What a dummy.

Allie smiled as Ben stopped in front of her.

"Hey," Ben said.

"Hey."

"He's crushing it," I whispered to Sammie. She looked unimpressed.

Nothing was happening. They were just staring at each other. Then I realized he was waiting for me to tell him what to say.

"What's up?" I said.

Ben followed my lead.

"Nothing," Allie said. "What's up with you?"

"Nothing."

"You going to the dance with anyone?"

"I'm keeping my options open. What about you?"

I had been anticipating that answer and said, "How about closing them and going with me?" It was a real killer move. I wished I had been that cool with Sophie. The only problem? The cellphone service in the school was notoriously bad. The connection was shaky.

Ben said, "How about a loser like me? Wait, what?"

"You're not a loser. You're sweet."

To make matters worse, Luke the Lurker slid up beside me and peeked through the trees to see what I was looking at.

"I'm gonna have to put a stop to that," Luke said.

"Don't be a jerk, Luke," I said.

Ben repeated it to Allie.

"Huh?"

"Oh, sorry. That wasn't meant for you."

"Who were you talking to?"

"Let him talk to her," I whispered to Luke.

"I want to know who she's going with," Luke said, walking around the tree and heading straight toward Ben and Allie.

"Incoming," I said to Ben.

Of course, he said to Allie, 'Incoming.'"

"What? Ben, are you okay?"

"Yes, fine. So, about the dance. I think we would have fun together," I said.

The phone apparently cut out again because I heard Ben say, "So, about the dance. We could rub our buns together."

Allie's face registered confusion. It was almost good that Luke showed up at that moment. Ben was struggling.

"Hey, Allie," Luke said as cheerily as he could.

"Hi, Luke," she said.

"I just wanted to see if you decided to go to the dance with anyone. My offer still stands."

"I don't know just yet. I'm waiting to see who sweeps me off my feet. I need to see how badly someone wants to go with me."

Ben and Luke looked at each other and each raised an eyebrow. The competition just got real. Or even realer.

And so did mine. Sebastian Carravone walked by, wearing a pin on his shirt with a picture of Mia and Derek on it.

14

L ater that morning, I bumped into Zorch, who was cleaning up something chunky from the floor. It didn't look pretty. Was it the meatloaf he ingested the day before? I wanted to keep moving for fear that it was smelly puke, but the poor guy needed help. No way I was going to help him with the puke, even though it did look better than yesterday's meatloaf.

"Hey," I said, holding my nose. You couldn't be too careful.

"Not puke, buddy."

"Oh, great. Did you ask Miss Geller on a date yet? You should ask her to chaperone the dance with you."

"Not yet," he said, not looking up at me as he continued to mop the floor.

"What are you waiting for?"

"The right moment."

"When's that gonna be?"

"I'll know it when I see it."

"See if from where? The lair?"

"Austin, these things are complicated. Maybe I'll email

her. It'll be easier to get out," Zorch said, his face lighting up.

"You gotta do it face to face."

"And by the way, I'm not always in the lair. And aren't lairs for evil villains?"

"Not always." Actually, I wasn't sure.

"Let me do it my way," Zorch said.

"Okay. You're the adult. I'm just the genius kid with the girl way out of my league." For now.

Zorch chuckled. "Sophie *is* way out of your league. Hmm. Okay. Thanks for the help. I'll figure it out."

I threw him a wave and shook my head as I left. Handling the adult romances was harder than it was for me with the dumb kids.

It was time for science with Sophie. I had been so busy handling everyone else's romances, my own relationship with Sophie was floundering. We hadn't really recovered from the secret admirer and kissing stuff. Even though it came naturally to me, I was going to make an effort to be extra cute, funny, and witty to put all that stuff in the past.

When I entered the class, I almost fell over in shock. Mr. Gifford sat in his chair, staring up at the ceiling. His shirt was untucked and stained, seemingly with lunch. He hadn't shaved and it looked like there was tuna salad stuck in his beard stubble.

"Mr. Gifford, what's going on?"

"My life is in shambles, Austin. Beyond repair."

"Why? What happened?"

"Madeline Funderbunk happened. She lured me in and then squashed me like a stink bug. And that odor you smell is the splattering of said stink bug's defense mechanism, the chemical compounds of trans-2-decenal and trans-2-octenal."

I was thinking it was probably the lack of a shower, but I

wasn't going to bring that point up.

"I told you she was a little bit full of herself."

"She has every right to be. That is some woman. I'm smitten."

"Sir, do you really think she'll go for you in...your current state? I think you have tuna salad in your beard."

"Probably," he said.

"How old is that?"

"Two days. How long do you think it's good for? I haven't eaten in a day."

"It's not!"

Mr. Gifford slipped from his chair to his knees. "Madeline. Oh, Madeline," he whined at the heavens above. "Why?"

"Sir, how well did you actually know her?"

Mr. Gifford paused his whining and looked at me. "I get

very attached." He looked at the room starting to fill up with staring students and stood up. "Well, that was embarrassing."

"Sir, the tuna."

"Right." Mr. Gifford picked the tuna salad off his face and popped it into his mouth. He shrugged, as I nearly vomited.

I headed back to my lab table. Sophie was there, staring at me.

"What. Just. Happened?" she asked.

I shrugged. "I'm not entirely sure. He's apparently devastated from Mrs. Funderbunk's rejection." I didn't know how to say it. I stared at Sophie for a minute, trying to get my nerve up.

"Is something wrong? Are you okay?"

Dayna interrupted, "Hey Soph, Alvin. I'm trying to come up with a couples' name for Brad and me. What do you think of Brayna?"

I almost died laughing at the idea that the combination of those two could ever include the word 'brain' in it.

Sophie shot me a look and said, "It's okay."

"How about Bradya? Daybrad?"

"Keep working," Sophie said.

Dayna shrugged and continued on to her seat.

I wanted to continue our conversation. "Everything's fine. I miss you. I've been running around like crazy trying to help everyone get dates for the dance. I feel like we haven't seen each other."

"Well, we have the interview with Calvin later. The contest is starting."

Ugh. I forced a smile. "Can't wait."

∿

AFTER SCHOOL WAS OVER, I met up with Ben in the Atrium before everyone headed out to the buses. I had to stay after for the contest interviews. He wasn't happy.

"I totally botched it. Again," Ben said. "And Luke got Allie flowers, so I'm doubly worse."

"It wasn't your fault," I said. "We had a technology snafu. Bad connection." I wasn't going to tell him that if he could've just come up with the words, 'Do you want to go to the dance with me', none of that would've happened, but his confidence was already low. I learned from our Battle of the Band days that criticism wasn't going to help.

"Still. Normal kids can do it."

"You almost had it. Just ask her straight out."

Sammie walked over as we talked.

"Hey, guys. What's going on?"

"Just prepping him for another attempt at asking Allie to the dance."

"Oh," Sammie said. "Maybe you should move on. Ask someone else."

"Who? There's nobody else."

"We're sticking with Allie." I looked at Ben and said, "I told Amanda Gluskin Luke was looking for a date to the dance. He's gonna be tied up for a while. Maybe literally."

"Or in the Camel Clutch," Sammie said.

"That could happen to anyone," I said, defensively. If you heard my story about the Science (Un)Fair, you probably remember why I would feel that way. I pointed across the Atrium. "Dude, she's over there. Go."

"How do I look?"

"Handsome," Sammie said. She fussed with his hair.

"Wish me luck," Ben said.

"Good luck," I said.

"Wait! What am I gonna say?"

"Just say, 'It's about time you close your options and go to the dance with me.'"

"You sure?"

"Yep." Nope.

Ben took a deep breath, turned, and headed toward Allie.

"Our boy is growing up," I said, laughing to Sammie. She stared at Ben as he walked away. I had never seen her look at him that way before. "Oh. My. God. You like him."

"Do not," Sammie said, defensively, and with a punch to my arm.

"Oww," I said, rubbing my arm. "I saw the way you looked at him."

"You're totally wrong. He's like my best friend."

"He's my best friend," I corrected her, "so he can be your boyfriend."

"I've never liked him like that."

"Things change," I said, shrugging with a smile.

"It would be weird."

"Why? It would be so cool. You would be like Ron and Hermione!"

"Oh, so you're Harry Potter and Sophie is Ginny?"

"Uh, yeah."

"You're the Harry Potter of nerds."

"Oh, because Ron and Neville are so cool? I'm Harry Potter. Period."

"Careful or I might give you a scar. And it won't be as cool as a lighting bolt."

"Maybe you're not Hermione. Maybe you're Voldemort."

"You speak his name?"

"Always. I told you. I'm Harry Potter."

Of course, Randy just happened to walk by at that exact moment and laughed. "Hey, Harry Farter!"

15

The beginning of the contest started off fabulously well for me. My secret admirer had apparently struck again. Out of the corner of my eye, I saw Sophie storming toward me, a giant wad of crumpled red and purple construction paper in her hands. She threw it at my feet.

"Umm, hi. What's that?" I asked.

"Your secret admirer decorated your locker!"

"I can't control what other people do. I don't even know who it is."

"Whatever," Sophie said.

"Couples' interviews start in thirty minutes back here," Sophie said. "Do you have your tie?"

"Yeah, it's in my backpack."

"Put it on. I have to go fix my hair." She turned and walked toward the gym locker room.

"Good talk," I said. I looked at Sammie. "Can you help me out here? Why is she getting so mad? I didn't do anything."

"She's not mad at you. I think she's jealous."

"Of what?"

"I don't know."

"That doesn't make any sense."

"That's women for ya," Sammie said.

"Yes, it is," I said, nodding.

~

I STOOD with Sophie in the Atrium, as a crowd rushed outside. "You gotta see this!" someone yelled. "Everybody, come on!"

I grabbed Sophie's hand and led her outside. I wished I hadn't. I looked up into the sky to see a plane skywriting. It said, 'I love you, Reagy Weagy!' I felt my lunch backing up on me.

"What a waste of sky ink," I said.

"You know, it wouldn't hurt you to be more romantic," Sophie said, annoyed.

I wasn't sure if she was really mad at me or just that we were upstaged in the contest we thought we already won.

Once we got back in, the couples' interviews were ready to start. Sophie headed over to me as I sat on a bench watching Calvin's camera crew get set up. She looked beautiful.

"Hey," I said. "You look beautiful. Your hair came out great."

"I don't really like it, but I guess it's good enough. Sorry about before. I know it's not your fault."

"It's okay. Sammie said you're just jealous," I said without thinking.

"Of what?" Sophie asked, defensively.

"She didn't know. It's one of the great mysteries of life," I said, smiling. "Let's just have fun. And hope that Calvin and/or Randy end up in the Camel Clutch."

"I may be the one to do it," Sophie said, fire in her eyes. Uh, oh.

One of the producers walked over to us. She was probably my mom's age, with frazzled black hair and glasses. She wore a headset and held a clipboard.

"You two are Sophie and Austin, right?"

"Yes," Sophie said.

"Well, you're up first. Just be yourself. Calvin is...really good."

Ummm, no. Well, I guessed it depended on what she was talking about. Good at what? Embarrassing himself and his interviewees? If that was it, she was absolutely correct. I was nervous. I didn't like Calvin Conklin. He was a total idiot. Kind of like Randy, only dumb. And he was unpredictable and wacky. I was concerned about what he would ask us. There was basically a 99% chance that he would embarrass Sophie or me.

The producer ushered us over to Calvin as he readied himself for the interview. There was a leather chair for him and a matching love seat for Sophie and me. There was a giant sign behind us advertising the TV and radio station sponsors.

We plopped into the love seat, Sophie sitting closest to Calvin.

The producer said, "So, here's how this works. Calvin will interview you and everyone else. Then anyone who wants to go to the website can watch the interviews and vote on the cutest couple. Those scores will be part of your overall score that will include the other events as well. Got it?"

Sophie and I both nodded.

Calvin looked at us and asked, "What shouldn't I ask you?"

Sophie shrugged and looked at me.

"I don't know. I guess don't ask me if I ever wore a diaper to win Sophie over," I said, laughing.

"Right. That's embarrassing," Calvin said.

The producer looked at Calvin and asked, "You ready?"

"Just have to warm up my eyebrows real quick." Calvin proceed to raise and lower his eyebrows in unison and then singularly. He looked at me and asked, "The girls love it when you can make your eyebrows dance."

"I'll keep that in mind," I joked.

Sophie shot me a look.

Calvin said, "Here we go."

The camera man said, "We're shooting in 3-2-1."

Calvin looked into the camera and said, "Hello, there. I'm Calvin Conklin, superstar reporter from Channel 2

News, but I'm sure you already knew that. I'm here at Cherry Avenue Middle School interviewing some Gophers for the Cupid's Cutest Couple Contest. No, not actual gophers. That's their dumb mascot's name."

Calvin shrugged and continued, "Be sure to check out all of our interviews on our website and vote for your favorite couple. Or don't. I don't really care. They'll pay me regardless. And I make bank, people." Calvin touched his earpiece. "Yes, Ted? I know we talked about this. I thought I was doing a good job this time. So, you're saying no? This is hard, Ted. I don't see you out here doing this. Oh, we're still taping? Oh, right. Let me get back to it. You know, you're not perfect, either. You interrupt me a lot. Oh yeah, still taping."

I adjusted my tie, loosening it. I figured I might need some extra flexibility if I needed to make a run for it.

Calvin continued, "So, I'm sitting here in front of our contest winner, Sophie Rodriguez and she's with Austin Davenfart. Strange name, but one of the other contestants told me that's how it's spelled."

I looked over to see Randy and Regan cracking up like idiots. I rolled my eyes.

"Tell me, what nationality is that? It's very unique."

I looked back at Calvin and said, "It's Davenport and it's English."

Calvin looked confused. "I know we're speaking English, but where does the name, Davenfart come from?"

"It's Davenport and it comes from England," I said through gritted teeth.

"Oh, right. I've heard of that place. This is riveting stuff. Here's how the contest works. There are four events. Today is the interview, which will be voted on by fans. Each couple will be ranked based on their performances. The winners will receive five points and the next place will receive one less until we get to the last place, who will receive one point. We add up all the points over the four events and then name our winner. Easy peasy."

Sophie looked at me and smiled. We were gonna crush it.

"Okay. Let's get going here. My first question is, have you ever worn a diaper to win Sophie over?"

Ugh. What an idiot. I was talking about both Calvin and me. "I umm, well…"

"No," Sophie said at the same time I said, "Yes."

"Which one is it?" Calvin asked.

I said, "No," as Sophie said, "Yes."

Sophie huffed.

"Interesting. Tell me, how did you two meet?"

Sophie answered, "School. We were in science class together."

"We have good chemistry," I quipped. I heard a few chuckles, but it didn't register with Calvin.

"Oh, I would've thought you met online, you know with all those dating apps."

"We're twelve," Sophie said, forcing a smile.

"Yeah, right. Have you guys, you know, smoochie smoochied?" Calvin asked, holding the microphone in front of Sophie.

Sophie's face went red.

"That's none of your business," I said. "Next question."

"That's what people who haven't smoochie smoochied say."

Before I knew it, the interview was over and Sophie was a thousand times more angry than when we started.

I grabbed her arm as she started to storm off. "Maybe it'll be better than we think."

"How?"

"Editing?" I said.

"Are they going to edit us out of the interview entirely?"

"You never know with Ted," I said, unhelpfully.

Sophie pulled her arm away and completed her storming off.

The producer walked over to me and said, "I thought that went rather well."

"What interview were you watching? Calvin's horrible. I'm gonna get dumped if we don't win this contest."

"Yeah, probably," she said.

Lionel Lamar was up next with Kara Wendell. Lionel wore a simple t-shirt and shorts, with flip flops. He seemed to wear that type of outfit regardless of the weather. His long, blond hair was tied back in a pony tail. Kara wore a yellow dress with black shoes. Her black hair was up in a bun.

Calvin kicked off the interview with a question to Lionel. "So, tell everyone how long you've been together."

Lionel leaned back into the love seat and put his arm around Kara. She looked like she might explode with excitement. Lionel said, "Time is just a construct, dude. I just live in the present moment, man. And live each fabulous day with this wonderful young woman to the fullest."

Calvin held the microphone in front of Kara. She just giggled. Hearts were basically flying above her head as she looked at Lionel.

"How do you deal with the drama of middle school romance?" Calvin asked.

Lionel leaned forward, "It's like surfing, bro. You just take each wave as it comes. Sometimes, you ride off into the sunset. Other times, you face plant and eat sand. You just get up and try again, man."

Kara looked like she was going to pass out.

Calvin asked, "Tell me how you first met."

Kara just giggled again.

Lionel spoke up and said, "The sun was setting after a long day on the ocean. The waves got the better of me. As I walked through the warm sand toward the parking lot, I saw a vision of beauty. I felt an immediate attraction. A pull toward her. I built her a sandcastle that we had dinner in and we've been together ever since."

So, we totally lost that round. I didn't even want to tell Sophie about it. She would find out soon enough once the voting started. I was just angry that he gave them such easy questions when he clearly tried to make mine difficult. I mean, who asks someone to tell them what they don't want to talk about and then asks them that very question? Idiots. That's who.

I did decide to stick around for Randy's interview on the off chance that something would go wrong. Typically, everything bounced in Randy's direction, but once in a blue moon, he got what was coming to him.

Randy and Regan sat in the love seat next to Calvin, their smug faces beaming for the camera.

Calvin looked into the camera and said, "We're back with Randy Warblemacher, star athlete, and Regan Storm, cheerleader. It's like a storybook relationship." Calvin looked over at Randy and said, "That's all well and good, but you have to be able to get through the difficult times. Tell me, have you ever farted in front of each other?"

I almost died laughing. I couldn't wait to see how Randy answered the question

Randy scoffed, "I've never farted in my life. Period. End of sentence."

"Not even a little squeaker?" Calvin asked.

"No," Randy said, forcefully.

"Not even one that's silent and doesn't smell?"

"No."

"What about a burp?"

"That question doesn't even deserve an answer."

"Well, I give you a lot of credit. Channel 2 News did a study that showed that 40% of marriages ended due to excessive farting. I'm not sure if they broke it down between the big, wet ones, the squeakers, and the silent-but-deadly ones, but be sure to check that one out on our website." Calvin held his earpiece. "No, Ted. The people want to know." He looked at Regan. "Besides not farting in front of each other, even though I'm not convinced he's telling the truth, what's the secret to your relationship?"

"Looks," Regan said. She looked into the camera and winked.

"I hear you on that. All my relationships are built on looks."

"And that's why you're single, right?" Someone heckled from the crowd.

"It's my own choice!" Calvin yelled, defensively. Calvin continued, "Now where was I? Talking about my good looks? No, not that. Oh, I know!" He looked at Randy and Regan. Randy's smirk had disappeared, replaced by a frown. I felt really bad for him. Well, not really. "Why should you win the competition?"

Regan said, "I already answered that. Looks." She shook her head. "I mean, honestly."

I couldn't stick around for the rest of the interviews. It was too embarrassing. The thought of Derek and then Ditzy Dayna with Brad Melon getting interviewed by Calvin Conklin would normally be great entertainment. I would love to see Derek and his dumb butt chin crash and burn, but I didn't wish an interview with Calvin on anyone.

16

I tried to call Sophie that night. I texted her, too, but I got no response. I was frustrated that she was angry at me. First, because of the secret admirer nonsense. Then Calvin and his ridiculous interview. None of it was my fault, but I was losing my girlfriend over it. The whole thing wasn't fair. I needed to put a stop to it. But how?

The next morning didn't help make the situation any better. I forgot that the interviews were related to the contest for a minute or maybe I had pushed the whole thing from my mind. When I got into the Atrium, Sophie was standing with Just Charles. At least she was waiting for me. She could storm off at any moment, but it was a good start.

"The polling scores are in," Sophie said.

"Good morning to you, too," I said. It didn't help.

"I'm in third place behind Kara and Regan. It's so unfair. Their interviews were so easy."

"What place am I in?" I asked.

"You know what I meant," Sophie said.

"That's the way the cookie crumbles," Ben said.

Sophie just stared at him.

Just Charles, thankfully, changed the subject. "Cheryl's late. She didn't say she wasn't coming to school."

"Was she feeling okay?" Sammie asked.

"Last I checked, yes. She should be here. I'm nervous."

"I talked to her last night," Sophie said.

That hurt. She wouldn't take my calls, but she talked to Cheryl? It was worse than I thought. I had been through that before and it usually didn't end well.

Everybody looked around.

"There she is," Ben said.

Cheryl was walking toward us. Just Charles looked over, relieved. And then got even more nervous. Lincoln Madison stepped out of a crowd, stopping in front of Cheryl. They talked for a second. She grabbed something from him and put it into her pocketbook and continued walking over toward us.

"Uh, oh," Just Charles said.

"Hey, guys," Cheryl said.

"What did Lincoln have to say?" Just Charles tried to ask, as laid back as possible.

"Nothing much. I told him I was on my way to see you guys."

"And what did he give you?" Just Charles asked, a little more pointedly.

"A note. I guess I'll read it later."

"Why read it at all?" Just Charles asked.

"Because that would be rude."

Relationship tension was building everywhere. I didn't know it at the time, but another note would be waiting for me at my locker.

When I got to my locker and opened it, the note fell out onto the floor. Just Charles bent down to pick it up.

"Not again," I said. I quickly scanned the hallway to see if anyone was waiting for me to find it. It didn't seem like it.

"What is it?"

"A note from a secret admirer. Sophie's getting all crazy about it." I grabbed the note and slipped it into my pocket.

"This whole place is getting V-Day cray cray."

"Ain't that the truth, Ruth," I said.

"It's Just Charles," he said.

"I know, dummy. I was rhyming. Never mind." I stopped before we headed into Advisory. "You know what?"

"What?"

"I haven't gotten detention in a while. I think it's time I got one."

"What? Why?"

"Don't worry. I always have a plan."

"I trust you. And as long as I'm not getting detention, I'm fine with whatever you do."

"Thanks for your support. I'll see you later. Just tell Mrs. Callahan."

"Yep," Just Charles said, disappearing into the classroom.

I hurried down to the Main Office. I wanted to beat the start to the morning announcements. My whole plan was based on the element of surprise.

I slipped into the office. Mrs. Murphy looked up at me while she was on the phone and smirked. Apparently, they still expected me there often.

There were a few students and teachers in the office, but nothing crazy. Nobody who would try to stop me. I glanced into The Butt Crack. Ms. Pierre wasn't there. Everything was falling into place.

I walked slowly past the front desk, toward the Speaker of Doom. It was now or never. I was going to tell my secret admirer to back off. I was taken. Sophie was my girl and that was that.

Stephanie Lang paced in front of the Speaker of Doom. Apparently, she was going to make some sort of announcement as well. Hers was sanctioned, but still. I didn't think she'd mind if I went first.

I slipped in front of Stephanie, switched on the Speaker of Doom, and spoke the following words, "Good morning, Gophers. This is Austin Davenport. I have a special announcement. I have a secret admirer..." And then everything went to poop.

Before I could finish my speech, professing my love to Sophie and telling my secret admirer to shove those notes where the sun don't shine, a Chinese throwing star hurdled through the air. It whizzed past my ear and sliced the main wire that ran out of the microphone and up into the ceiling. Sparks flew as I jumped back.

I turned to see Ms. Pierre, still in her follow through, admiring her handy work. She straightened her suit jacket and said, "In my office, Misterrrr Davenport."

My heart felt like it was going to implode. I didn't care that I was about to get detention. I was immune to those and fully expected to get in trouble. The only problem was that I expected to get into trouble after I was done delivering my message. Not in the middle. And Sophie was not going to be happy. Lunch was going to be a war zone. Maybe even worse than the Meatball Mayhem food fight that I started last quarter. Not to mention, I think I almost just died.

I followed Ms. Pierre into The Butt Crack. It was dark. She flipped on the lights as she entered.

Stephanie smiled at me and said, "Thanks."

"No problem. Glad I could help you." While ruining my own life.

"Sit down," Ms. Pierre said, simply. "What do you have to say for yourself?"

"I'm sorry?"

"Doesn't sound like it."

"I needed to set the record straight on something, but it totally backfired. How many days detention do I get for this?"

"You seem to not care about getting detention. I've been through your files. I've had extensive conversations with Principal Buthaire. And I've studied you while you sleep."

"Wait, what?"

She continued without explaining how or why she watched me sleep. "You can either have ten days detention for that stunt, even though it will hurt my statistics, or you can drop out of the contest, which I know means a lot to you."

She wasn't exactly right. The contest didn't mean

anything to me. I wished it never happened. But Sophie meant everything to me. Quitting the contest would be the end to my relationship.

"As horrible as ten detentions sound, I'd rather not disappoint Sophie, so I'll take the detentions."

"Twenty detentions it is, Misterrrr Davenport."

"What happened to ten?" I yelled.

"Watch your voice with me. I will not stand for it. That decision was entirely too easy for you to make. Ten detentions wasn't a deterrent at all."

"It had nothing to do with the detentions and everything to do with Sophie."

"Oh. I wish I had known that before. It could've saved you ten detentions."

"Well, can't you just change it?"

"We have a strict no take-back policy."

"That's ridiculous," I said. "There's no such thing as no take backs outside of the playground."

"Oh, there certainly is. Do you think you can return half-eaten meatloaf at the cafeteria?"

"No," I said. I wasn't going to comment on the fact that nobody was stupid enough to eat half of the meatloaf. Well, except for Zorch, but as we established, his whole nasal system was lost in the war. "Can I go, now?"

"Yes, you're late. I'd hate to have to give you more detentions."

I ran out of The Butt Crack as fast as I could, nearly knocking over Dr. Dinkledorf on the way out.

As I was walking to class, I saw my idiot brother and his butt chin. He looked pained. It was odd. He normally looked like a smirking doofus like he knew he was cooler than you or at least he was thinking it. I wasn't sure if I should stop and see what was wrong or let him be a normal kid with frustrations and anxiety like the rest of us, but I wasn't a heartless jerk like he was.

"What's wrong?"

"Mia. Things are going too fast. She wants to share locker space. That's a big deal. I'm not sure I'm ready for that kind of commitment."

"Dude, I thought you had a real problem. I don't have time for this nonsense. I've got real relationship problems."

"Yeah, what the heck was that?" Derek asked.

"Ms. Pierre cut out the speaker before I could finish."

"That stinks, but back to me. What if she's a slob? What if she eats my protein bars?"

"That's your biggest concern?"

"It's like the adult equivalent of moving in together."

I just shook my head and walked away while he was still talking about his locker problems and protein bars. I think he had been hanging out with Mr. Muscalini too much.

～

I TRIED to find Sophie after first period, but she didn't take her normal route through the east wing stairs, so I missed her. It wasn't the worst thing in the world. I hoped she would calm down a little by the time I saw her in third period at lunch.

After the second period bell rang, I grabbed my stuff and was the first kid out of the classroom. I hustled down the hall, bobbing and weaving as well as any nerd could, navigating the packed halls. I wanted to get there early and hopefully fix things with Sophie before everyone was inside the cafeteria.

My plan didn't work. She never showed up. I sat with Ben and Sammie, picking at my food.

"Has anyone seen her?"

"No," Sammie said. "She's probably pretty upset. You botched that one pretty bad."

"Yeah, dude. Even I could've done better than that," Ben added.

"You don't think I know that?" I said, annoyed.

"Sorry," Sammie said, also annoyed.

I took a deep breath. "No, really. I'm sorry. I'm just worried and really frustrated. That wasn't how it was supposed to go. I didn't get a chance to finish. I was going to tell my secret admirer I was taken and to back off, so Sophie would feel better."

"Now she thinks you like the attention," Ben said.

"Thanks. I hadn't thought of that."

"Sorry."

"No, I'm sorry," I said.

I took out my phone and held it underneath the table. I texted Sophie, 'Where are you? Ms. Pierre cut me off. Didn't get to finish. Wanted to say to back off.'

I sent it and then quickly added, 'back off to the secret admirer. I wanted her to know I was yours.'

I waited all period and got no response. None of my friends saw her for the rest of the day. She didn't answer any of my texts or anything from Sammie or Cheryl. I had a flashback to the time I pulled an all-nighter on Sophie's lawn to get her attention. I hoped it wouldn't come to that this time. I wasn't ready for the emotional trauma of wearing a diaper again.

As I sat in science class, alone at our lab table, I'd had enough. My stomach was in knots. I felt like I might puke. I was worried about Sophie.

Randy kept looking over at me and mouthing, "I have a secret admirer." And then laughing. He wasn't helping, but when did he ever? He didn't, in case you didn't know the answer to that question.

I stood up as Mr. Gifford spoke. His beard was growing rapidly and I think he had yesterday's lunch in it again. At least he was cutting down the amount of time his lunch stayed in his beard. Last time, the tuna was in for two days.

I heard my phone ding. I slipped it out of my pocket and glanced at it from underneath the table. It was from Sammie. It read, 'Soph went home sick.'

Sick of me, probably. I picked up my books and walked toward the back of the classroom.

"Austin, where are you going?" Mr. Gifford called out.

"I've got to find Sophie. I can't talk about earthworms anymore."

"But I was just getting to the best part!"

～

I CUT the rest of school. The only other time I had done that was in the beginning of sixth grade when I had just met Sophie. I needed my sister's advice on what to do about my feelings for Sophie. It was also science, which Mr. Gifford understood. It was also the key factor behind Mr. Gifford making me his relationship guru, which I regret to this day.

On my way out of school, I saw another Mia and Derek pin. I remembered what Sophie had said about being more romantic. I decided to take it to the next level. I texted Cheryl as I walked out the door, 'Does your dad still run the print shop? Can you print up some posters of me and Soph and put them up around school?'

Anyway, I slipped out of school undetected. I half expected Ms. Pierre to repel off the roof in mountain climbing gear and tackle me before making it to the edge of school grounds, but thankfully, that didn't happen.

I hustled home as quickly as I could. It was less than two miles, but running that wasn't exactly easy for a nerd like me. I took a few breaks, stopped for a Gatorade and some candy at the convenience store, and made it home within a half hour. School was at least still in session.

My mom wasn't home, so I grabbed my bike out of the garage and headed over to Sophie's. I was a little sweaty and I got chased by Mrs. Wagner's dog, Lucky, but besides that, I made it to Sophie's house in one piece.

Whether or not I would leave that way was an entirely different story. And may or may not involve the fire department and other municipal and government agencies.

I walked my bike up Sophie's driveway and parked it in front of the garage door. There weren't any cars on the driveway, so I wasn't sure if they were home or not. I headed up the steps to the front door. I had been in this situation before. If you never heard the story about how we met, I once slept on a chair outside Sophie's house overnight, refusing to leave until she talked to me. It worked. I hoped I wouldn't have to resort to such measures again, but I was willing to do what it took. That's when I wore the diapers that Calvin so rudely mentioned.

I took a deep breath and rang the doorbell. A dog barked and then the door opened. Sophie's mother stood in the doorway and forced a smile.

"Hi, Mrs. Rodriguez. I know Sophie's not feeling well, but I really need to talk to her. Is she here?"

"She is. She's pretty upset."

"I know, but you have to believe me that it was a big mistake. I didn't get to finish what I wanted to say."

"You don't have to convince me," she said. Mrs. Rodriguez called over her shoulder, "Sophie, Austin's here to see you."

"I don't want to see him," Sophie called back.

I took another deep breath, as Mrs. Rodriguez and I looked at each other awkwardly.

"Based on our history, I'm sure you already know that I'm not going anywhere. I don't have any diapers, but I'll get some. I just hope it doesn't have to come to that."

Mrs. Rodriguez tried to hold in her laugh, but couldn't. I had cracked Sophie's first line of defense. She turned around. "Honey, just listen to what he has to say."

"Fine," Sophie said, annoyed. Footsteps stomped all the way to the door.

Mrs. Rodriguez slipped away as Sophie stood in her place, her arms crossed.

"Hey?' I said.

Sophie didn't answer.

"Ms. Pierre threw a ninja star across the office and it cut out the Speaker of Doom before I could finish what I had planned to say."

"You expect me to believe that? The principal had ninja stars?"

"It's true. I swear."

"Yeah, right," Sophie said, closing the door in my face.

I knew she wouldn't open the door again if I rang the bell nor pick up the phone or answer a text. I didn't know what to do. I had no diapers, nor did I have a place to take off my underwear to use as a slingshot. If you don't know that story, don't ask.

The dog kept barking, which kept me from being able to concentrate. The dog! I remembered Baxter had a doggie door to go out into the backyard from the kitchen. It was my only shot. I might end up in the Jefferson County Prison System, but I had to take that chance. It probably wasn't much worse than middle school.

I walked to the side of the house and listened at the gate to make sure Baxter wasn't outside. I quietly opened the gate and slipped into the backyard. I navigated a few spots that looked like poop and found myself at the kitchen door.

I pretty much had no idea what to do at that point. I couldn't just crawl in through the door, grab a snack, and sit down at the kitchen table. But what? I took a deep breath and knelt down. I pulled the doggie door open and called inside, "Hello? Please, Sophie! I'm begging you. The speaker cut out before I could tell my secret admirer that I was taken."

"Go away," Sophie said. "I don't want to see you."

"When have I ever lied to you?"

She didn't answer. I wasn't sure if she was calling the

cops, just ignoring me, or if she left and was watching Ellen or something else on TV.

I stuck my head through the doggie door to see where she was. I scanned the kitchen. She wasn't there. There was a hallway that led into the den, but I couldn't see all the way down the hall. The angle wasn't good enough. If I could just reach a little farther inside, I thought I might be able to catch a glimpse. I shimmied forward and got my shoulders through and then my arms. I craned my neck and saw straight down the hall into the den.

It was a success. Well, the viewing part. The rest? Not so much. What was the problem, you ask? I was totally stuck.

I heard footsteps coming my way through a different entrance to the kitchen. I thrust my arms forward and used my hands to push my body back through the doggie door. My shoulder jammed into the side. I turned, shifted, exhaled every ounce of air I had in my body, but it was of no use. I was stuck.

"Austin?" Sophie said. "Austin!" she yelled, angrily.

I looked up at Sophie, forced a smile, and said, "Hey! What are you doing here? Can't believe we bumped into each other like this."

Baxter must've heard my voice and zoomed into the kitchen. He slid to a stop right in front of my face and started licking me like I was a giant ball of peanut butter. It must've been my sweat or something.

I was busy trying to get Baxter to stop when I thought I heard Sophie laugh.

"Baxter, please. You're not the Rodriguez I want to kiss."

"You're lucky my dad's not here," Sophie said, chuckling. "Mom! Austin's stuck in the doggie door!"

"That's nice, honey. Wait, what?"

Mrs. Rodriguez ran into the kitchen, her eyes bulging.

"I can explain," I said.

"Let's worry about explanations later," Mrs. Rodriguez said.

Well, at least there was some good news.

"Can you move forward through the door?" Sophie asked.

I tried it, but it was no use. "My hips are stuck."

"We're gonna have to call the fire department," Mrs. Rodriguez said.

"No," I said, quickly. "I can get out. I got in, right? Which was an accident, by the way."

"You fell through the doggie door?" Sophie asked.

"It's a long story," I said, squirming, but making no progress.

"Should we call Daddy?" Sophie asked.

"Ummm, no," I said. "I'd rather the fire department."

They both laughed.

"Seriously, though. You can't get out?" Mrs. Rodriguez asked.

"That depends. Do you have seventy-four sticks of butter?" I asked, as Baxter sat on my face. Things just kept getting worse.

"Baxter!" Sophie said, picking him up, and laughing.

"Should I call your mother?"

"She doesn't have that much butter, so I vote no," I said.

Both Sophie and her mother were cracking up. "Sorry," Mrs. Rodriguez said. "I'll call the fire department."

I looked up at Sophie. "We still have game night tonight."

"Can we make it in time?" Sophie asked.

"I'm not sure at the moment, given the circumstances. I guess it depends on how quickly the fire department gets here," Mrs. Rodriguez said.

Within twenty minutes, two ginormous fire trucks showed up, sirens blaring, and escorted by a fire responder car. It was totally unnecessary. They couldn't have taken a nondescript van or something?

"Do you want water or something?" Sophie asked.

"No, thank you. I might have to pee eventually."

"Good point. No diapers," she said, trying not to laugh.

"I'm glad this is so funny to you," I said, trying not to

laugh. I actually was glad. Saustin was back! That was our Hollywood couple's name. Try to keep up.

A fireman in full gear stomped through the kitchen followed by another man running behind him in a first responders uniform. He was sweating and looked visibly upset.

"Come on, McGuire. I'm supposed to go first."

"Sorry, Fontana. Didn't know," McGuire said, shrugging.

"Didn't know? It's in the name, first responder. You guys always do this to me," he whined. "You don't see me trying to do your job."

"Can we help you, gentlemen?" Mrs. Rodriguez said.

"Sorry, ma'am," McGuire said. "We'll take care of this. I just have to call it in."

Fontana shot McGuire a look. McGuire corrected, "He's going to call it in."

Fontana pressed the button on the radio attached to his jacket. "This is Officer Fontana. We got a code forty-two here."

"What's a code forty-two?" Sophie asked.

"Idiot kid stuck in a doggie door," McGuire said.

"There's a code for that?" I asked. "And I'm not an idiot."

"There's a code for everything," he said. "And have you looked at yourself in there?"

"Point taken," I said, hanging my head in shame.

McGuire bent down and inspected my head and shoulders, and then the doggie door frame. He looked back at Mrs. Rodriguez. "Ma'am? How much butter do you have?"

"How much do you need?"

"Seventy-five sticks?"

"Oh! So close, Austin!" Sophie said.

"Not helping. But just out of curiousity," I said to McGuire, "Are you rounding up?"

He didn't answer as he grabbed my ears and pulled.

"Owww!"

"Yeah, we're gonna need the butter."

"Sorry, we don't have that much," Mrs. Rodriguez said.

"How about a jug of olive oil?" Fontana asked.

"No way!" I yelled.

"What about that baby butt paste?" McGuire asked. "Your face does look a little rashy."

"Bigger no! And it's not diaper rash. It's embarrassment."

"Yeah, it looks it. Well, we're gonna have to knock the door down, then."

"What?" Mrs. Rodriguez nearly lost it.

"I'll pay for the butter out of my allowance," I said.

McGuire cocked his head and said, "Do I know you? Hey, aren't you the lead singer for Mayhem Mad Men?"

"I am," I said, ashamed. I was dragging my band down with me, too.

"My kids are huge fans. They're gonna love this story." McGuire took out his phone, leaned his face down next to mine, and said, "Smile!"

I forced a smile as the flash nearly blinded me.

"Should I go to the store and get butter? Are you serious about that?" Mrs. Rodriguez said.

"Firemen don't kid about butter, ma'am. I'm sure you can understand why."

None of us knew why.

"I didn't know that was a thing," Fontana said.

"You're not a fireman."

"Can we hurry this up?" I asked. "Sophie and I have to win game night for the Cupid's Cutest Couple Contest."

"Depends on how fast the butter gets here," McGuire said.

"We're really doing the butter thing?" I asked.

"Baxter is gonna have a field day on you," Sophie said, laughing.

We waited for about twenty minutes when Fontana returned with two shopping bags filled with sticks of butter. He dropped them on the table and said, "We've got to throw this into the microwave and we'll be good to go."

Mrs. Rodriguez got to work on melting the butter.

I looked up at Sophie, who was still laughing, by the way, and said, "My phone is in my pocket. I don't think I can reach it. I should probably call my mother."

"I'll dial for you." Sophie grabbed the house phone, punched in some numbers, and held the phone up to my ear.

McGuire crouched on the other side of me, a bowl of melted butter in his hand. He inspected the situation.

"Hey, mom. No, I'm fine. I slipped up. Forgot to tell you I wasn't coming home. Just contest stuff. No, you don't have to go to the game night. Bring your video camera? Please, mom. No. Don't try to butter me up."

Sophie laughed.

"You want me to stop?" McGuire asked.

"I'm not talking to you," I whispered and then continued talking to my mom, "That was Sophie. No, I don't know why she thought that was funny. No, she doesn't have a man's voice. There's something wrong with the connection." I grabbed the wrapper from the butter that was on the floor and crumpled it up next to the speaker of the phone. "Don't show up tonight. Gotta go. Bye." I hung up the phone.

It took about thirty minutes of buttering, maneuvering, whining, and pulling before McGuire pulled me through the doggie door with a pop. I flopped onto the kitchen floor while everyone else cheered. I put my head in my arms and hid in shame.

Sophie looked at the clock and said, "We have to be there in twenty minutes. We're never gonna make it."

"For the lead singer of Mayhem Mad Men, we can make it," McGuire said.

"Don't forget, she's our lead guitarist," I said.

"Oh, yeah," McGuire said. "We should go."

"How are we getting there?" I asked.

"In style," McGuire said.

$\sim$

McGuire was right. We pulled up into the parking lot outside the gym entrance in style. Sophie and I rolled up in a fire-engine red fire truck, lights flashing, sitting in the front seat with Sophie in between McGuire and me.

Do you want to know the best part? McGuire cut the engine and asked "You guys want to blow the horn?"

"Umm, yeah," Sophie said.

Sophie reached for the horn, but I grabbed her hand.

"I wanna do it," she said, annoyed.

"You can, but you should wait five seconds."

"Why?" she asked. And then she smiled and counted, "Three. Two. One," and then pushed the horn.

Randy was walking with a group of people about twenty feet in front of the fire truck when the horn blared a deep honk. He jumped back, a look of horror on his face, like he just realized he pooped in his pants in front of the entire school, which might actually have been the case. Once he composed himself, he glared at us through the window. It was one of the most satisfying moments of my middle school career.

"That felt so good!" Sophie said.

"I think he tinkled in his shorts," McGuire said. "I do that to Fontana at least once a month."

A crowd gathered around the fire truck. McGuire hopped out of the driver's side of the truck and said, "It's been fun, kids. Good luck with the game and with the band. And for some reason, Austin, I have a strong desire to eat popcorn."

"Good one. A butter joke. I probably won't hear any more of those tonight. Thanks for the help."

"Yeah, thanks," Sophie said.

I opened the door and hopped off the side of the truck into the crowd of people. I turned back and held out my hand to help Sophie, but she just jumped down unassisted. I was used to it at that point.

"Why does it smell like an extreme amount of butter?" some dude asked, pinching his nose shut.

"You say that like it's bad," I said. "It's a new cologne. Everybody wants to smell like butter."

I walked through the crowd with Sophie and into the hallway outside the gym.

The producer from the interview with Calvin and Channel 2 News was waiting for us inside. She ushered us into the nurse's office, just across the way from the gym, which was flowing with people.

"Right this way. You'll hang out here until we're ready to start. You're not allowed to see the first game in advance."

She held the door for us as we entered. The rest of the contestants were already inside.

"Ugh, Davenfart. You reek. I mean, worse than normal," Randy said.

"What is that?" Regan asked, seemingly like she was going to throw up.

"I kinda like it," Ditzy Dayna said.

"Yeah," Brad said, looking at me. "Do you mind if I lick you?"

"Umm, yes," I said.

Brad leaned forward, tongue out.

"I mean, yes! I mind!"

"Oh, that's disappointing," Brad said.

Thankfully, the producer changed the subject. "Everyone's parents sign their waivers?"

"Yep," I said.

Everyone else nodded in agreement.

"Okay. So, I won't go through this long list of safety precautions because you foolishly signed away your rights, and the news station and the school have a fart-ton of insurance."

The producer grabbed a small cardboard box and pulled out five blindfolds. She tossed them to each of the boys.

"You'll put these on when it's your turn to go. Tonight's

contest is an important game of partnership. There is an obstacle course that the boys must navigate blindfolded."

"Whoa," Lionel said.

"But you will have a guide." The producer pointed to all the girls. She then looked at all us boys. "How well your guide communicates and how much you trust your guide will help determine how quickly you finish the course. Once you've completed the course, you can watch the other participants. You will be judged only on the time it takes to complete the course. Good luck. Sophie and Austin are first in five minutes."

I looked at Derek, Randy, Lionel, Brad and then Sophie. I leaned in and whispered, "Sorry in advance. Feats of physical prowess are not my specialty, even when I can see."

Sophie nodded. "We'll do our best," she said. She sounded a little annoyed. I didn't think it was at me, but more at the contest.

"Don't slip up, butter boy," Randy said.

"Shut up, Randy," Sophie said.

"Don't tell my boyfriend to shut up," Regan spat.

"I'll tell whoever I want to shut up. You can shut up, too."

Regan and Sophie stepped toward each other, both seemingly trying to obliterate the other with lasers from their eyes.

My idiot brother yelled, "Chick fight!"

"Whoa, there's no need for that," Lionel said, jumping in between the girls. "It's bad mojo."

I grabbed Sophie's arm and pulled her back. She moved toward me, continuing to stare down Regan.

Brad said, "I like that word. Mojo." He said it fast, "Mjo." He said it slow, "Moah...Joah." He said it repeatedly, "Mojo. Mojo. Mojo. Mojo."

We kind of all forgot the almost chick fight, wondering how Brad had made it that far in life already.

The producer returned and said, "Blindfold on, Austin."

As I put the blindfold on, Lionel said, "Good luck, dude."

"Thanks," I said, nervously.

"Don't embarrass the family," Derek said.

Randy said, "Too late. He exists."

I couldn't see anything. All I heard was Sophie roar, "Aaaaaahhhh!", the scuffling of sneakers, and then a crash.

I tore off the blindfold to see Randy doubled over, holding his stomach, while Brad and Lionel held Sophie and Regan from tearing each other apart. There was a lot of jostling, grunting, and yelling.

Derek again yelled, "Chick fight!"

The producer yelled, "Enough! This is supposed to be fun."

Randy said, "That was a cheap shot, right in my solar plexus."

Ditza Dayna looked at Brad and said, "Solar plexus. Sooolaaar plehhhxusss. That's fun, too."

The producer grabbed Sophie by the arm and said, "Let's go."

When we got out into the hallway, I put on my blindfold as I said, "Thank you, but you didn't have to do that. Let's just do what the producer said. Have fun."

Sophie said, angrily, "Yep. Sounds great."

If you haven't noticed, Sophie has a competitive side. Sometimes it was helpful. Other times, not so much.

Sophie led me into the gym by my arm. As we entered, the crowd started cheering. It sounded like a lot of people. I almost wished I had a diaper.

"Oh, no," Sophie said under her breath.

"What?" I asked, nervously.

"Nothing," she said.

"You can't say, nothing, while I'm blindfolded and my life is on the line!"

"Your life is not on the line. Most likely."

"I'm a nerd in the gym. My life is always on the line!"

"Okay, we're at the start of the course. There are a few balance beams, some cones and a scooter or something. A football ladder. A rope swing."

"Sounds lovely," I said.

Then I heard Calvin Conklin's voice say, "It is time for our first contestant here at the Couple Olympics. The object is to navigate the obstacle course as quickly as possible. Our first couple is Sophie and Austin!"

The crowd cheered and yelled out a lot of encouragement and also a few negative things.

"He's gonna die! I hoped he told his parents he loved them."

"The poor nerd doesn't know what he's gotten himself into."

"He's going to get dumped after this."

It was very helpful for my confidence. My pulse raced like crazy as I waited for Calvin to kick things off.

"About five feet in front of us is a balance beam on the floor. I'll guide you across," Sophie said.

Calvin yelled into the microphone, "Help me count them down! Three! Two! One! Go!"

I took a few big steps and then Sophie yelled, "Stop! Now, step up, left foot."

I stepped up onto the balance beam and wobbled as I squeezed Sophie's hand, using her to steady myself.

"Small steps. Just one foot in front of the other."

I could do that. I took it slow, heading across the beam

with relative ease. The crowd cheered after I hopped off the beam without breaking my face. I was feeling confident.

"Good job. Okay. Now, we have to climb over a beam about chest high.

Sophie pulled me toward it quickly. I ran with my other hand out, feeling for the beam.

"Okay, use both hands to climb over."

I felt the beam with both hands in front of my chest and then gripped it. I jump and tried to swing my right foot over the beam.

All I heard was Sophie say, "Owww!" as my foot connected with something.

The crowd groaned.

Calvin said, "Oooh, that's gonna leave a mark."

"Are you okay?" I gasped as I struggled to get yourself over the beam.

She didn't answer.

"Sophie?"

"Glad they signed those liability waivers!" Calvin yelled into the mic. "This place is a death trap!"

I tore off my blindfold and searched for her. She was sitting on the floor, coming to her senses. She looked up at me. Blood trickled from her lip. In her hand, she held two teeth. And on her face, she held anger.

So...it was the second time we got to meet Fontana, the First Responder. Unfortunately, McGuire was replaced by an EMT, a Mr. Jenkins. And the butter was replaced by blood, so that was also unfortunate. I wondered if I would be replaced as well.

17

The next morning was almost as wacky as the night before. Sophie was getting two shiny, new teeth at the dentist office and wouldn't be in school. Oops, again.

As I headed to gym, I bumped into Cheryl. "Posters are up!" she said, excitedly.

I had totally forgotten about the posters with everything that had happened. "Awesome! Thanks. I hope she likes them when she gets back."

"She will," Cheryl said, heading on to class.

She didn't. But I'll get to that later.

I headed straight to the locker room and got changed for gym class. As if the prospect of getting my butt whipped in gym wasn't bad enough, as I was leaving the locker room, I passed Mr. Muscalini's office and saw him wiping his tears.

I wanted to ignore it and keep moving. I had enough problems as it was, but he looked up to see me.

"Davenport, I, umm, I was just giving my tear ducts a workout. I believe in taxing the body's entire system, including my automatic nervous system."

Even though he was lying, I was at least impressed he knew some biology. "Sir, is everything okay?" I asked.

"It's the Romans! The blasted Romans," he said.

"What are you talking about?"

"The Romans gave us gladiators and for that, I will always be grateful. But they also gave us Valentine's Day," he said, drying his eyes.

"Did Brody's mom dump you?" He was dating my former camp counselor and band manager's mom.

"With the strength of the great gladiator, Spartacus, she stabbed me through the heart and left me to die," Mr. Muscalini fell to his knees and began to cry again.

I patted him on the shoulder. "Sir, can I ask a question?"

Mr. Muscalini stopped crying and looked up. "Davenport, that was a question."

"Another question?"

"I guess," he said.

"I never understood why someone with your impeccable nutrition was with someone who was a pie-eating champion."

"What's the question?" Mr. Muscalini asked.

"Oh, right. How did you get along when you were so different?"

"Opposites attract, Davenport. You don't choose who you fall for. And I fell hard. It's not often someone has thighs thicker than mine. Once you see a woman squat 500 pounds, you'll understand."

"I don't think I ever will, but okay."

Mr. Muscalini looked up at the rafters in the ceiling. "Who gets dumped before Valentine's Day? Everybody wants to be a couple on Valentine's Day. I'm the lowest of the low. These biceps won't be dancing this year. And my quads, well, they won't see the light of day for a long, long time."

It was really touching, but I saw an opportunity that I couldn't let slip away. "So class is canceled then?" I asked, my fingers crossed.

"Davenport, I'm putting you in charge. I'm going to kneel in the middle of the gym and you are to instruct the class to pummel me with dodge balls until I fall unconscious."

"So, you admit that dodge ball is punishment?"

"It's character building," Mr. Muscalini countered.

Ugh. I was never gonna win that battle. But still it would be fun to throw stuff at Mr. Muscalini. I thought about putting Randy out there as well, but thought that might be an abuse of my power. It was a gray area.

18

I left gym class on a relative high. Everybody was thanking me for letting them pummel Mr. Muscalini, as if any of it was my doing. I usually got blamed for stuff I didn't do, so I decided to enjoy it while it lasted.

I was heading down the east hallway on my way to class. When I turned the corner, Zorch was waiting for me.

"Hey, buddy. I'm gonna do it."

"Do what?" I asked.

"Ask Miss Geller. She should be heading down the hallway in two minutes."

"Alright. Good luck."

Zorch waited patiently for a minute and then said, "There she is. Here I go." He took a deep breath and started walking toward her.

I watched as Miss Geller noticed Zorch, gave him a big smile, and then frowned, as Zorch continued to walk past her. She stared at him for a moment and then turned and headed back in the direction she was going. I slipped past her, noticing that she was carrying a rose in her hand. I was really confused.

I hurried down the hall to catch up to Zorch. It wasn't hard, even for me. He moped down the hallway, hanging his head. I slowed down as I caught up to him.

"What happened?"

"She's taken," Zorch said, glumly.

"What do you mean?"

"Somebody already asked her. She had a rose."

"I'll figure it out," I said, having no real idea as to how I was going to figure it out.

As I continued on to class, I bumped into Just Charles.

"What's the matter?" he asked.

"I'm stressed, dude! I'm trying to make everyone else's relationship work while my own is in the toilet. I kicked Sophie's face in. Who does that?"

"I can't help with that, but...Luke's getting his ear pierced after school. I'm going with him," Just Charles said, chuckling. Yes, he was okay with chuckling. You just can't call him, Chuck.

"Are you serious? I would love to see that," I said.

"Do you want to come and watch?"

"I wouldn't miss it for the world. I can't wait," I said.

"Oh, no," Just Charles said, his smile disappearing.

"What's the matter?" I said, turning around.

Cheryl was walking down the hallway with Lincoln. She smiled at him as he waved and headed into class. Cheryl walked up to us.

"Hey, guys. What's up?"

"Nothing," Just Charles said. "I'm late for class. See you later."

Cheryl and I watched Just Charles mope away.

"What's up with him?" Cheryl asked.

"I think his mother dropped him as a baby," I said.

Cheryl laughed. "Seriously, though. I don't know what's going on with him."

$\sim$

WE WERE at the mall after school. Mrs. Hill, Just Charles, and I stood next to Luke, who sat in a chair inside The Piercing Pagoda.

"You sure you want to do this?" Mrs. Hill asked.

"Definitely."

"It hurts," Mrs. Hill said. "I still remember when I got mine done."

"Please, Mom. I'm a man. I probably won't feel anything."

A young woman walked over with a gun-like device. Her name tag said, 'Harper.' She smiled at Luke and said, "We're locked and loaded. It's gonna pinch as the earring is shot through your lobe. Do you want to hold your mom's hand?"

"No!" Luke yelled, defensively.

"Okay, suit yourself," Harper said with a smirk.

Harper sanitized the target area and then held the piercing weapon up to Luke's left ear lobe.

"Are you ready?"

"I was born for this. Fire when ready, soldier," Luke said like a hotshot.

Harper pulled the trigger on the piercing gun. There was a quick pop of air as the earring shot out of the device and pierced Luke's ear.

And then there were the piercing shrieks of the man who was 'born for this.' Luke hopped off the chair as if he were blasted by a maniac bull and sprinted in a circle around The Piercing Pagoda.

"My ear! My ear! I think you blew the whole thing off! Is

it still there? Allie will never love me with only one ear!" Luke yelled, as he continued to run.

We all laughed, including Mrs. Hill. She called after him, "We can't see it while you're still running." Then she looked at us and asked, "This is about a girl?"

Just Charles nodded. "I'm afraid so."

"I should've known," she said, shaking her head and chuckling.

Half the store was staring at Luke as he fell to the floor, writhing in pain, still clutching his ear.

A tiny girl, no more than four-years old said, "Mommy, why is that boy acting like a baby?"

"That's how they always act. Your father hasn't grown up, either."

"Are those tears?" Just Charles asked, taking a closer look at Luke's face.

"No," Luke whined.

"Those eyes are looking watery," I added.

"No, they don't," Luke whimpered.

"Watch this," Mrs. Hill said to us. "You guys want some milkshakes?"

"Milkshake?" Luke said, like he was on his deathbed. "I might be able to get one down."

~

THE NEXT MORNING in the Atrium, Allie walked up to our group and admired Luke's earring up close.

"I love it. You look so tough."

"I know," Luke said. "I did it for you."

"That's so sweet," Allie said. "It's so shiny." She reached up and touched his earlobe.

Ben didn't look happy.

"Yowww!" Luke said, spinning away from her.

"What was that?" Allie asked, as the rest of us laughed.

Luke stuttered, "I'm...just... just so excited that you like it. I was dancing."

Ben looked at Allie and said, "Whatever. I'm gonna pierce my belly button for you."

"That's just weird," I whispered.

Allie seemingly didn't know what to say. "Oh, well... that's interesting. I...gotta go."

Ben and Luke both spat out super quick goodbyes with the hopes of beating the other.

As Allie walked away, Sammie looked at Ben and said, "I don't think that's the best idea. I'm sure we can come up with something better."

"Chicks dig belly button piercings."

"Yeah, for themselves," I said. My sister and most of her friends had them.

"You guys don't know anything," Ben said. "She said I was interesting."

"No, she said that your strange belly button gesture was interesting, which was a nice way of saying you're an idiot," Luke said.

"Okay, Mr. Yowsers," I said. "You haven't set any IQ records in the last twenty-four hours."

~

THE NEXT DAY, the drama intensified. I was hanging out in the Atrium with Ben and Sammie. As Just Charles and Luke walked over to us, I noticed Luke's earring was nowhere to be found. Instead, he wore a giant white bandage, not just on the lobe itself, but his entire left ear.

"What happened?" Sammie asked. Ben and I were too busy hiding our laughter.

"They said I might lose the ear," Luke said, shaking his head.

I noticed Ben's face stiffen. I looked up to see Allie approaching. She was looking at Luke's ear.

"Oh, you poor baby," Allie said.

Luke looked over at Ben and cracked a tiny smile. He looked back at Allie with a pained look on his face and smiled weakly.

Allie continued, "Unfortunately, it doesn't look that tough anymore. That's disappointing."

Ben broke out into a smile.

Luke was flustered. "What? Really? But it hurt so...I mean, what can you do? It probably won't be the last limb I lose."

We all just looked at each other. I wasn't sure where Luke got the idea that losing limbs was manly. Or that ears were limbs.

"Hey, Hill," Mr. Muscalini called.

Luke turned around.

"You get ear implants or something?" Mr. Muscalini asked.

"Ear implants? No, just an infection."

"Flesh eating bacteria?"

"No," Luke said, concerned.

Mr Muscalini said, "Well, whatever it is, we can build a training regimen to whip that ear back into shape with high impact interval training and a high-protein diet."

Mr. Muscalini's answer to everything was more protein. Broken arm? Eat some chicken. Late for class? Amino acids. Car won't start? Protein shake in the gas tank.

I looked at Just Charles. Normally, he would be joining

in on the fun. Everybody loved giving Luke a hard time. But his face was stone. I watched him as he took a deep breath and took a few steps toward Cheryl.

"Hey," she said to him.

"This isn't working out," Just Charles said, his voice shaking.

"What's not?"

"This."

"This what?"

"This relationship."

"Really? Are you dumping me?" Cheryl asked, her volume rising.

Just Charles looked around to see a growing number of people looking their way. He whispered, "That sounds kind of harsh. Maybe we can call it an uncoupling?"

"Ugh, you're such an idiot," Cheryl said, stomping away and wiping tears from her eyes.

"Uncoupling? What the heck is that?" I asked.

"I read my mom's Cosmopolitan magazine. I should probably stop doing that."

19

My whole crew of friends was silent. If you've been around us for a while, you know that's not a normal occurrence. I was the first to say something. It wasn't overly helpful, but it was something.

"Did you just dump Cheryl Van Snoogle-Something?" I asked.

Ben said, "What are you doing? That was the dumbest thing I've ever seen."

"Me, too. And Derek is my brother. And then there's Luke…"

Just Charles' face went pale. "What did I just do? Should I ask her back out? No, I can't. She'll think I'm flaky."

"She already thinks you're an idiot," Sammie said.

"Tell her you had a brain fart," I said.

"I don't want to tell her my brain farted. What can I do?"

Sammie comforted Just Charles, while Ben just shook his head.

"I don't get it," Ben said. "If I had Allie, I could never do that."

Sammie said, "Can I say something?"

"What?" Ben asked.

"I'm not sure Allie's right for you."

"Why do you think that?" Ben asked, annoyed. His face was turning red as he waited for a response.

Sammie fidgeted. "She just seems to be enjoying the attention-"

"Because she likes me," Ben interrupted.

"She likes the idea of guys competing over her."

"Yeah, of course. How could anybody ever like me? Is that what you're thinking?"

"No, that's not what I meant at all," Sammie said.

Ben walked off in a huff.

"You're totally jealous," I said to Sammie. "I mean, you're right, but you're jealous, too."

"No," she said, defensively. "I mean, no, I'm not jealous, but I'm right."

"Are you sure?"

"Positive," she said.

I saw something in her eye that told me she was not at all positive. It had to be weird. We had been friends for all those years. It would probably be pretty weird for me if someone I had been friends with my whole life suddenly became more than a friend to me, like Sammie.

"I think you want to smoochie smoochie," I said and then followed with huge, exaggerated kissing sounds.

She punched me on the arm, the universal sign that I was right.

"Yep. Confirmed with embarrassed punch."

"You're just embarrassing yourself."

I shrugged. "What else is new?" I nodded in Ben's direction and said, "Let me go see how he is."

I walked over to Ben, who was sitting on a bench across the Atrium, under one of the dogwood trees. A leaf twirled out of the air above me and landed on the bench. I glanced up into the tree and did a double take. I initially thought I saw Ms. Pierre up in the tree, but when I looked the second time, she wasn't there.

I shook my head. I was going crazy.

Ben shook me out of my stupor when he asked, "What's cooler than an earring?"

"A tattoo," I said, not really thinking.

"Well, I'm getting one. I think Allie would love it."

My brain kicked in. "A tattoo? You're twelve. You have to be an adult."

"I bet I could get one in Mexico. Or prison."

"Do you want to go to either of those places?"

"Not really."

"So, I think you should pass on the tattoo. Maybe some ripped jeans? A faux hawk?"

"Not good enough. It's gotta be big. Maybe I should just beat up Luke in front of her."

"That's something Derek would do."

"Good point," Ben said, scratching his head.

Sophie walked over with a rose and a note in her hand. She had a cut on her lip and it was a bit swollen, but she had two new teeth, so she would be totally fine.

"Are you okay?" I asked.

Sophie smirked. "I'll be fine."

"Sorry again," I said, ashamed.

"It was an accident," she said, but seemingly not convinced she was good with that explanation.

"What's this all about?" I asked, pointing to the rose. "Is that for me?"

"Umm, no," Sophie said. It was a dumb question. Typically, girls don't get you flowers after you knock their teeth out. You should probably make a note of that. Sophie continued, "I found a rose sticking out of my locker and then a note inside as well."

I took a second to recover from the hurt and concern about new competition. After a moment, I said, "Being that you read mine, I think it's only fair."

I held my hand out and she handed it over. I opened it and started to read, "Dearest Sophie." I looked up at her, "That's pretty formal. Seems like a real dud." I continued reading, "Your eyes are like the ocean. When I look at you, I feel like I'm drowning. When you laugh, I pretend it was from something I said. When you sing, it sounds like it's coming from the heavens. Oh, to know you. To hold your hand. To feed you pizza." I frowned at her. "That's kind of weird, plus he's probably not talking about Frank's."

"When was the last time you wrote me a love letter?"

"When have you written to me? I won the contest for you."

"The contest we're losing?"

"That's not fair. That's Calvin's fault."

She walked away in a huff.

I hesitated for a moment, not sure what to do, and then chased after her, but she slipped into the crowd heading to Advisory and I lost her. Perhaps forever. Too dramatic? You'll just have to wait to find out.

20

I was back to focusing on the adult romances. Kid romances were so dumb. I had a lunch mission to accomplish, well, besides getting Sophie unmad at me. The problem was that she skipped lunch. Who does that? Usually, kids at Cherry Avenue skipped the period after lunch on account of the day's less-than-special lunch special.

I was still trying to get Zorch a date with Miss Geller. I had to find out what the deal was with the flower. I waited patiently on the hot lunch line as she dished out heaping plates of lobster thermidor. Just kidding. It was salmon patties. Yep, the school had resorted to selling us big ol' stinky fish burgers. They probably got a great deal on bulk salmon or maybe even bought them used.

I stepped up to Miss Geller's and asked, "So, I saw you with a rose."

"Yes. It was pretty, right?"

"Definitely. Who was it from?"

"It was from me."

"Huh?"

"I got it for Mrs. Westerman. Her husband died over the summer. I thought she could use a pick me up around Valentine's Day."

"Oh, that's great news," I said, excitedly.

"That her husband died?" Miss Geller asked, surprised.

"Oh, no. That's terrible. I was talking about you being single."

"That's great news? Austin, I'm a little too old for you and I thought you had a girlfriend."

I felt my face flush red. "No, not for me. I mean, you're a lovely woman and all, and make great...food, but it was for Zorch." That's the last thing I needed: Rumors that I asked the lunch lady out on a date. "Remember, I told you I think he liked you? I think he wants to ask you to the dance, but he thought that someone else had already beaten him to it. He saw you with a rose."

"Oh, I had no idea," she said, blushing.

"You should be a chaperone at the dance with him."

"Okay. You'll tell Eugene about the rose?"

"Definitely," I said, trying not to puke as my salmon cake seemed to move.

On my way to see Zorch and tell him the good news, I passed Randy in the hallway.

He called out to me, "We're gonna smoke you like a salmon, Davenfart."

I shrugged. "I don't even know what that means, but it sounds fishy. And I don't know why you're talking trash to me when the surfer dork is winning."

"Surfer dork, I like that, Davenfart. I'm gonna use that."

He couldn't have called me Davenport just that once?

∽

I DECIDED to take Derek's advice. Practice for the next session of the contest. That would also give me some time with Sophie, which would be good after all the ups and downs we'd been having. After she calmed down following the love letter debacle, she agreed to join me at my house.

Sophie and I sat on the couch in my den. It was cramming time. We were practicing for the next session of the stupid Cupid contest, the Newlywed Game. The basic gist of the game was that we would be asked questions about our relationship and each other and we both had to come up with the same answer.

"We have to crush everyone in the next round," Sophie said. "We've been together longer than any of the others by a long shot. We need to catch up."

"You're right. Let's do this," I said.

"What's my great aunt Rosa's birthday?" Sophie asked.

"The one in Puerto Rico?" I asked.

"No, the one in California."

"Don't you think we're getting a little too crazy here? Do you really think Calvin is gonna ask that?"

"Maybe you're right. What's your third favorite color?" Sophie asked.

"I don't have one," I said, shrugging.

"You have to have one! Do you wear boxers or briefs?"

"Calvin is going to ask about my underwear? Everybody knows the answer to that, anyway. They saw my Batman briefs during the Santukkah! musical."

"Oh, right," Sophie said. "What are your parents' names?"

"Mom and Dad," I said, simply.

"Okay, good. Mine, too."

"What do you want to be when you grow up?" I asked.

"President. You?"

"An entrepreneur. Maybe a rock star. Perhaps a rock star entrepreneur."

"Pick one," she said.

"Rock star entrepreneur."

"Is that even a thing?"

"Absolutely. Favorite author?" I asked.

"Come on, really?"

"Yeah, dumb question." We both knew it was C.T. Walsh.

The rest of the practice session basically went like that. I don't think we got a whole lot of actual practice in, but we had fun together, which hadn't happened for a while.

～

ON THE BUS the next morning, I looked out the window,

watching the cars drive by with old ladies yelling at us for driving too slow. It was relaxing.

Ben looked at me and said, "How are you going to handle Randy?"

"What do you mean?" I asked.

"I mean, he's going to cheat his face off. How are you going to stop him?"

"That's a good question," I said, tapping my lips. "Hmm, how would you cheat if you were them?"

"Well, how does the game work?"

"Dumb Calvin is going to ask a question. We both have to answer it and have the same answer."

"Like trivia?"

"No, more like stuff about our relationship. It doesn't matter who's right. It matters that we put down the same answer," I said. "So that's how they'll game the system," I continued.

"How?"

"They'll either have predetermined answers, which might be hard to do for such a wide range of potential questions. Or they could communicate answers to each other somehow after the question is asked."

"How could you do that?" Ben asked. "Hand signals?"

"You'd probably have to have a whole lot of stuff figured out before then, though."

"Right," Ben said, thinking.

"What if they had ear pieces?"

"Like Calvin does with Ted?"

"Yeah, but they can't talk. But someone else could just give them both the answer."

"That's it," Ben said.

"It could be like how I helped you ask Allie to the dance."

"You were helping?" Ben asked, his eyebrows raised.

"There were technical difficulties," I said and then changed the subject. "That's how they're gonna cheat. So, how do we take them down?" I asked, pounding my fist into my palm. "We've got 'em right where we want 'em." It was a little dramatic, but I rarely had Randy set up so nicely to fail.

21

It was time for the next chapter of Cupid's Cutest Couple Contest: The Newlywed game. The five competing couples stood just off the stage in the school's auditorium, just behind Calvin and Devi Divine. Ms. Pierre was out on the stage with a mic in hand.

"Good evening," Ms. Pierre said, enthusiastically. "I am Principal Pierre. We are very excited to have you all here for this special occasion. Tonight, we host Cupid's Cutest Couple Contest, sponsored by Channel 2 News W.S.T.I.N.K. along with everyone's favorite radio station, 102.3!"

The packed auditorium cheered.

Ms. Pierre continued, "Please give a warm Gopher greeting to 102.3's Love Hour DJ, Ms. Devi Divine!"

Harp music began playing over the loud speaker. Devi Divine, a tall woman with straight black hair, who wore a flowing white dress with gold accents, walked out toward Ms. Pierre. She looked like she was an angel. She strode out to cheers and stood next to Ms. Pierre.

Ms. Pierre continued, "And you all know Channel 2

News' most eligible bachelor and newscaster, Calvin Conklin!"

Calvin entered to more laughs than cheers and the laughter grew as more and more people realized what he was wearing. Calvin waved to the crowd and blew kisses, dressed as Cupid. He was shirtless, but wore white feathery wings, a halo, and some sort of diaper-looking underwear. He carried a bow and arrow.

Calvin grabbed the mic out of Ms. Pierre's hands and started speaking," Oh, you're too kind." Nobody was actually cheering.

He continued, "Welcome, lovers, gophers, and lovers of gophers. I'm Calvin Conklin, your host with the most... beautiful eyes. And I'm here with my co-host, the lovely Devi Divine. She is almost as heavenly as I am. At least that's what my mother tells me and she hasn't even seen me in this exquisite outfit just yet."

People yelled out from the crowd, "Put some clothes on!" and "You look like a giant baby!"

Calvin looked over at Devi and said, "Tell them why we're here tonight, Devi."

Devi stepped forward and smiled, "We are here this evening to determine Cupid's Cutest Couple."

Calvin cut her off, "I know what you're thinking. Devi and I are not competing, but we would make an amazing couple."

Devi looked like she threw up in her mouth.

Calvin glanced over at Devi and said, "She looks ill for some reason. I'm going to pass it over to her anyway, because that's what Ted told me to do."

"Thanks, I guess, Calvin. And he's right, for once. I was ill for a moment. The thought of the two of us as a couple makes me want to vomit." Everybody laughed except for Calvin. She continued, as Calvin looked like he might cry, "We're here to decide on who is...Cupid's Cutest Couple. And we've prepared five precious pairs to present to you."

"Let's bring them out now!" Calvin yelled. "Please give a warm welcome to Randy and Regan, Kara and Lionel, Sophie and Austin, Derek and Mia, and Dayna and Brad."

Each couple walked out holding hands to a cheering crowd. I looked around the auditorium. My heart started pounding at the sight of so many people. So many people who were going to watch me make an idiot of myself. The last time I was on that stage was for the finale of Santukkah! I had mixed feelings about the place.

Ten chairs were laid out in pairs across the stage. Sophie and I were in the middle. Sophie had Kara to her left and I had Derek to my right. Devi and Calvin were off to the side of us.

Calvin said, "If I'm not mistaken and I never am, don't we have two brothers in the contest tonight?"

Devi rolled her eyes. "That's right, Calvin. We have a sibling rivalry here. Austin and Derek are brothers."

"What? Really? They looking nothing alike. Austin has a rather nondescript chin while Derek has that fabulous butt chin like mine. Such depth to it. It's like the Grand Canyon. Have you ever been to the Grand Canyon before, Devi?"

"No. Let's move on."

"Maybe that could be our first date?"

"I'm gonna have to say a firm 'no' on that."

"Shocking, but okay." Calvin stepped toward the contestants. "Gentlemen."

Nobody looked at Calvin.

Calvin continued, "I'm talking to you, boys." We all looked at him. "You're up first. Everyone take a mini dry erase board and marker from the lovely Miss Divine."

Devi walked down the line of contestants, handing out the boards.

"What you're going to do for the first question is this. Write the name of your gal's most important distant relatives and where they live."

Yes! I wrote down, 'Aunt Rosa from Puerto Rico.'

We all finished writing our answers.

"Show us what you got!" Calvin yelled.

I turned my board over and looked at Sophie's. She had Aunt Rosa, but from California. Ugh.

Devi said, "Zero points for Brad and Derek. One point for Austin and Randy. And two points for Lionel."

Sophie looked at me and said, "I told you this stuff mattered."

"Sorry," I said.

"Another question for the boys. Have you ever farted in front of your lady friend?"

Ahhh, farts. Like for real. I didn't know what to write. I had farted in front of her once, but would she embarrass me by writing that down? I couldn't imagine she would do that to me.

"Okay. Turn 'em over," Calvin said.

My board said, 'no,' while Sophie wrote, 'yes.'

"Aww, come on, Austin!"

"Okay, so I lied, but I didn't think you would tell everyone."

Everyone else got one point. We were tied for last place, with both Randy and Lionel ahead of me.

"Ladies," Calvin continued, "what is his worst habit?"

I wrote, 'getting detention.'

"Show your cards, kids," Calvin said.

I turned mine over. Everyone started cracking up, but I wasn't sure what was going on. Sophie and I actually got one right as she wrote, 'detention.'

I peered over at Randy's board and it said, 'Austin is a loser.'

"What an idiot," I said.

The crazy thing was, though, that Regan put the same thing. They were definitely cheating. It was time to drop the bomb on them. I looked into the crowd and found Just Charles and Ben. I gave them the hand signal we came up with to implement our cheating plan. It was on.

Well, before it was on, Derek looked across at Randy's board and said, "Wait. I need to change mine."

"You can't change your answers, Derek," Devi said.

Derek didn't listen and wrote on his board, 'Austin pees sitting down.'

Everyone in the crowd was laughing and pointing at Derek.

"That has nothing to do with you or your relationship!" I yelled at him.

"I know," Derek said, smirking.

"That's not even a negative. Mom hates when you pee on the seat."

"I do not. I have exquisite aim."

"Yeah, right. Ask the potpourri. It's more like the pee pouri."

The crowd laughed. I wasn't sure if it was at me or Derek. I felt the dreaded warmth of redness rushing through my face.

And then I caught Ben in the crowd. He didn't look happy and he was giving me a thumbs down. My eyes bulged. Next to him, Just Charles was looking down into his lap and slapping something. I could only assume it was the signal jumbler that seemingly was not jumbling anything. We had Randy right where we wanted him, mid cheat, and we couldn't stop him.

"Okay, next question is," Calvin said, "what is your favorite food to eat together?"

"Hold on a second, Calvin," I yelled. "I need to change my last answer. The crowd chatter rose as I scribbled on my board.

Sophie whispered, "What are you doing?"

"Winning."

I held up my board, which said, 'Randy and Regan are cheating. Check their ears.'

Calvin read the sign out to everyone, "Randy and Regan are cheating. Check their rears? What the heck does that mean?" Calvin held his earpiece and said, "Ted, can I even do that? I don't want to check their rears. Can I get a no-rear-checking policy in my contract next time?"

The crowd laughed, while Randy's face went pale.

I said, "Their ears. Someone is feeding them answers."

Calvin said, "Oh, that makes more sense."

Devi walked over to Randy and Regan. Randy was angled in his chair toward Regan, one ear away from the crowd, while Regan had her hair down, which wasn't unusual.

Randy fidgeted in his chair, while Regan reached toward her ear and pulled out a wireless Apple earbud. The crowd reacted in shock.

"We're not cheating. This is to listen to music."

"And Randy just happens to be listening to the same music with the other ear bud?" I asked.

"Yeah, we do everything as a couple," Randy said, joining in on Regan's lie.

Even Brad thought it was unlikely. "Yeah, that seems pretty suspect."

Devi grabbed the ear buds and listened. "It's playing music," she said. "I don't think there is anything in the rule books specifically banning ear buds or music."

The producer lady from the other night walked briskly out onto the stage, followed by Ms. Pierre, who, of course, gave me a dirty look.

"Do you have proof that they cheated?" the producer asked me.

"Other than they both wrote that I was a loser when the question was about Randy's worst habit? Which is cheating, by the way," I said, staring at him

Randy made an 'L' out of his thumb and index finger and held it up to his forehead.

The producer looked at Ms. Pierre, who said, "If there's no proof and nothing in the rule book, we have to let them continue." Ms. Pierre turned to us and said, "Let this be a warning to you all. Anyone caught cheating will not only be thrown out of the contest, but will receive ten detentions!" She was seemingly only looking at me.

"This is unbelievable!" Sophie yelled to no one in particular.

"So unfair," Mia added.

I was so angry. The crowd booed as Ms. Pierre and the producer walked off the stage.

"Well, that was interesting," Calvin said. "I'm just glad I didn't have to check anyone's butt."

"Umm, yeah. Okay. Let's get back on track," Devi said, turning to the contestants. "Favorite food to eat together?"

The crowd was still pretty vocal, but we continued. Sophie and I got it right with pizza. I mean, if we didn't get that one right, there was no hope for us.

I looked over at everyone else's answers. Lionel and Kara both had the same answer, but I couldn't believe it.

Devi said, "I think we need some clarification here. Lionel and Kara both have New England clam chowder."

Calvin asked, "Is that the red or the white?"

Lionel and Kara scribbled their answers and showed them to the crowd. They both wrote, 'white.'

They were good. The crowd went nuts. Sophie banged her fist into her knee.

Devi asked, "What are you most likely to argue about?"

Whatdya know? Sophie and I both answered, 'the Newlywed game.' We got another point and gained on everyone else, except Lionel and Kara, who apparently don't argue at all.

Brad and Dayna both wrote, 'who farted?'

"You two love birds fight over who farted?" Calvin asked.

"No," Brad said. "Somebody farted."

Derek's face went red.

Devin said, "Moving on. What is your biggest fear, gentlemen?"

Of course, Randy and Derek both answered, 'none.'

I looked over at Sophie's board and she wrote, 'losing me.' Regan wrote the same thing. They were slipping without being able to cheat.

Her face went beet red when she read my sign that said, 'Farting in science class.'

"What? That's ridiculous," Sophie said, annoyed.

"I don't want to fart in front of you in science class, so I don't lose you. It's pretty much the same thing."

"No, it's really not."

Ahhh, farts, again, for real.

Devi said, "Here's a good one. Better get this right if you

know what's good for you, guys." She read the card in her hand and asked, "Where were you for your first kiss?"

"Ooooh, the first smoochie smoochie, eh?" Calvin said. "This is going to be interesting. Where do you think we'll be, Devi?"

"Neverland," Devi said.

Calvin pumped his fist, not realizing that Neverland was not a real place.

I wrote down, 'Frank's Pizza.' Sophie wrote, 'Ren Fair.'

"Frank's? That was on your cheek," she said, annoyed. "That wasn't real."

"It was to me."

"Ugh. We can't even get that right. We're doomed as a couple."

That didn't make me feel all that good.

Randy had, 'in my dreams.' Regan wrote, 'in his dreams.'

Lionel and Kara both wrote, 'sunset on the beach.'

Derek wrote, 'under the bleachers' while Mia wrote, 'TBD.'

If I hadn't been so worried that I was gonna get dumped in front of the entire audience, I would've laughed at my brother trying to fool everyone into thinking he had kissed Mia under the bleachers.

Calvin read a question card and said, "Uh, oh. This could cause some problems."

Ahhh, farts. I already had more than some problems. I didn't need any more.

Calvin said, "Ladies, what do your parents think of him?"

I wrote, 'Love me.' Sophie wrote, 'meh.'

"Meh? I'm hurt."

"You camped out on my front lawn when I refused to talk to you. It was kinda weird."

"You said it was cute."

"Yeah, but to parents, it's weird."

"And the fire department had to melt a thousand pounds of butter to get you dislodged from my doggie door."

"I thought I bonded with your mom over that," I said, disappointed.

"Yeah, but right after that, you kicked me in the face and knocked out my teeth."

The crowd laughed. I slumped in my seat.

"It was an accident."

Devi said, "Here's a fun one. Most embarrassing thing done in front of your lady friend, gents."

I wrote, 'Flashed Batman underwear.' Sophie's read, 'Showed underwear.'

I smiled at her. "We've still got a chance. We just need to go on a streak."

"Like the streaks in your underwear," Derek added.

"Not funny."

Randy wrote, 'nothing' while Regan wrote, 'Lost epic sword fight.'

"What?" Randy said. "You gotta be kidding me. I was double-teamed. They should've been disqualified."

That one felt pretty good because Sophie and I were the ones who beat him in the sword fight. Well, it was more Sophie than me, but still, it was a team effort as far as I was concerned. I did all the hard work. She just swooped in at the end. Anyway, it was good to see Randy on the defensive and the two of them on the outs.

Calvin asked, "Who is the better singer?"

I wrote, 'me' while Sophie wrote, 'tied'.

"Really?" Sophie asked, annoyed.

"I am," I said, defensively. "You're by far the better guitar player. But I'm the lead singer in the band. The band that you're in, too."

"I joined late. I could've been the lead singer."

"While we're on the topic of music, what is the favorite band you share?" Devi asked.

Sophie wrote, 'Goat Turd.' I wrote, 'Mayhem Mad Men.'

"How could you pick them over us?" I asked.

"Because that's our band. You can't be a fan of your own band. That's why I chose somebody else."

Randy and Regan both chose Randy's dumb band, 'Love Puddle.'

Apparently, Sophie was wrong. Your own band could be your favorite, but I wasn't about to tell her that.

Calvin looked out at the crowd and said, "I'd pretend that I did all the math myself, but you'd never believe me, so I'm just gonna be honest and tell you that Ted tallied up the scores and here's where we stand with one question left."

Devi said, "I think it's going to be close for a few of these happy, or seemingly not-so-happy couples."

Calvin said, "With eight points, we have the basement dwellers, Derek and Mia." He looked at Devi and asked, "Does Derek lose any points for the farting?"

Derek went red again. It was one of the highlights of the night.

Devi just shook her head.

Calvin continued, "It was a valid question. Anyway, Brad and Dayna have ten. Austin and Sophie have eighteen. Lionel and Kara have nineteen, while our top Newlywed couple, Randy and Regan, sit in first place with twenty-one points." Unfortunately, the early cheating helped them a lot.

"Okay. It's not as bad as I thought. We get one right and Lionel and Kara get it wrong, we can end up tied for second place," I said.

"Here's the last question of the night," Calvin said. "Ladies, what was your first impression of him?"

I wrote, 'quiet' while she wrote, 'cute.'

Sophie looked at my answer and grunted then stood up and stormed off the stage. I hurried after her, but she slipped out the back of the theatre and into the crowd that was flowing out into the Atrium. I lost her. I stood there among dozens of people, but so alone.

22

Sophie didn't respond to any of my texts or phone calls and it was too late to go climbing through doggie doors. Plus, my guess was that her father was home and he wouldn't be as enthused at my entrance. Not to mention, I heard the grocery store had butter on back order.

I looked for her in the Atrium before Advisory the next morning, but she was nowhere to be found. None of my friends had any good answers on what to do or how to fix things.

Not to mention, I had a poster problem. All of the posters of Sophie and me that Cheryl had put up had been defaced. My beautiful eyes had been cut out while Sophie had her two front teeth darkened, another reminder of my epic fail in the Trust game. Ben helped me take them down.

"Somehow, I'll get in trouble for this," I said, tearing down a poster and handing it to Ben.

He stared at it. "This has Randy written all over it."

"Ya think?" I said, annoyed. "Sorry. I'm just angry."

"I hear ya," Ben said, as we walked over to the last poster in the Atrium and ripped it off the wall.

For the last few minutes before we had to head to Advisory, I stood with Ben, Sammie, Just Charles, and Luke.

Just Charles stepped out from our pack, as Cheryl was walking in our vicinity.

"Hi," Just Charles said, nervously.

Cheryl ignored him like he wasn't even there.

Just Charles turned and watched her walk through the Atrium until she stopped in front of Lincoln. He continued to stare at her for a moment and then moped back to us.

"Do you think she's going to the dance with him? Do you

think they're dating?" Just Charles rubbed his face and took a deep breath.

"I didn't want to tell you this, but she is going to the dance with him," Sammie said.

"What have I done?" Just Charles asked the ceiling. "I Luked it!" He looked at Luke and said, "No offense."

Luke shrugged, then patted Just Charles on the shoulder and said, "Yep, you really screwed that one up, bro."

"Thanks for the support."

And then Allie walked up and made matters worse. It was a banner morning for relationships in my crew. "Hey, guys," Allie said to Ben and Luke. "How's it going?"

"It would be better if we knew who you were choosing for the dance as your date," Luke said.

"Oh, well, I've decided that I can't decide. I'll save both of you dances. I know you'll keep an eye out for me." She smiled and waved, then walked back the way she came.

"Is she serious?" Sammie said.

Ben and Luke just stared at each other.

"I've had enough drama for a lifetime," I said. "I'm outta here."

Just Charles joined me on our normal trek to our Advisory class. Neither of us said anything.

I turned the dial on my padlock and popped it open. As I opened my locker, another note fell out. I really wasn't in the mood for my stupid secret crush.

"What's this?" Just Charles said, picking up the note.

"Just deal with it. It's my annoying secret admirer. Trying to ruin my life."

Just Charles opened the letter and read it. "Umm, dude. This isn't from your secret admirer. It's from Sophie."

"What?" I grabbed the letter from him.

"It's not good."

I read the letter. I'll spare you the details. Saustin was no more. Sophie dumped me. And even worse, told me that it was best if we didn't speak to each other anymore. Tears welled up in my eyes.

Just Charles asked, "Dude, are you okay?"

I couldn't speak. I didn't know what to do. I felt like my heart had been ripped out of my chest by Amanda Gluskin and Camel Clutched until it popped.

I closed my locker and leaned my head up against it. I felt my breakfast oatmeal churning in my stomach.

"What do you want to do?"

"I think I'm gonna hurl," I said.

"Is there anything else you'd rather do?" Just Charles asked, unhelpfully.

"No," I said. "I've never wanted to hurl so badly before in my life. I want to be a professional puker."

"Not sure that's a thing."

"Don't crush my dreams. I'd like to try."

"How about I take you to Nurse Nova and you can do it there rather than on my shoes?"

"Okay," I whimpered. "Unless we see Randy or Regan on the way."

"Deal."

23

I spent the next three periods in Nurse Nova's office. She couldn't get in touch with my mother to pick me up, so eventually my oatmeal settled down and I no longer wanted to take my puking talents to the pros. I did, however, want to avoid lunch and Sophie. I wanted to talk to her, but I didn't know if I could do it without crying or otherwise embarrassing myself. Plus, she said she didn't want to talk to me, so I didn't want to make things worse.

Ben texted me during lunch. 'Dude, where are you?'

'At nurse. Almost puked.'

'Why?'

'Sophie dumped me.' It was hard to press send. It sort of made it official.

'What????? She's not here. What did she say?'

I couldn't rehash the whole note, so I just sent him a snapshot of the whole thing.

After a minute, Ben responded with, 'This is so crazy. So sorry.'

'I don't know what I did. I hate this stupid contest.'

'Should we take it down?'

'I can't get myself to leave the nurse's office. I don't think I have it in me.'

"If you can text, you can go to class," Nurse Nova said.

"My thumbs are ready, but the rest of me isn't."

"Very funny, Austin. You can rest a little while longer, but you should head back to class when you can."

"My pinkies are feeling pretty good, too, if you're keeping track."

Nurse Nova smirked. "I'll put that on your chart." She did not do anything of the sort.

I eventually headed back to class to try to finish out the day. I wasn't sure what to do about science class, but I figured I could always go back to the nurse's office if I needed to. The next few periods were a dreary blur. I don't think I paid attention to one word that was said. I just kept my head down and did my best to avoid eye contact with anyone, while trying to calm the swirling thoughts of hurt and dread in my head.

After fifth period, I moped down the hallway and caught Zorch in the corner of my eye. He stood in a little alcove by the stairs. I wasn't going to stop, but he called out to me.

"I'm gonna do it, Austin," Zorch said, clutching a broom.

"Sweep the floor?" I looked over, confused. "I didn't know you had to psych yourself up for that, but okay. I'll help. You got this," I said with some meh.

"I was talking about asking Miss Geller to the dance," Zorch said, chuckling.

"Oh, right. You got that, too."

"She walks down this hallway every day on her break." Zorch nodded his head down the hall. "There she is."

"Go get 'em, tiger," I said, faking a smile.

Zorch took a deep breath and started walking toward Miss Geller. He stopped dead in his tracks. I was afraid he lost his courage. He turned to me and said, "Broom or no broom?"

"Huh?"

"Should I hold the broom or not?"

"I'll take it," I said.

Zorch held the broom out for me. "This a very special broom, Austin. Take good care of it."

"I will," I said, trying to pretend that he wasn't crazy.

They were only feet apart when they stopped to talk. I couldn't hear what they were saying, but she was smiling and then Zorch fist bumped some kid passing by, so I was pretty certain it was a success.

Zorch rushed back to me like he just won the lottery. "She said, 'yes!'"

"Yeah, I've been telling you she would."

"Here, let me get that from you," Zorch said, holding out his hand for the broom. "I've been to war with this broom. It's helped me out of more jams than you could possibly imagine."

I couldn't imagine pretty much any jams that would create war that would be solved by a broom, but I let him have that one. It was a big day. Well, for him at least. Everyone else I knew was crashing and burning, including myself. And it wasn't over.

24

On my way to history class with Dr. Dinkledorf, Derek's girlfriend, Mia, tapped me on the shoulder.

"Hey, Mia," I said, monotone.

"Hey, Austin. I need some help. I don't know how to say this, but..."

"What's the matter?"

"It's about Derek. I know he's your brother and all, but I was hoping you could help me figure him out."

"I'm a genius and I haven't been able to figure him out," I said. "What's the problem?"

"He doesn't seem that into me."

He probably wasn't. It wasn't necessarily her fault. I hadn't seen him really interested in a girl, maybe ever. I didn't know what to say. I shrugged and said, "If that's how it feels, maybe it's true." I wasn't really in the mood.

"It just seems that he likes the idea of having a girlfriend, but not actually having one."

"It's a strange conundrum, but yes. That sounds about right."

She looked disappointed, so I didn't want to tell him about all the hamsters that we had that died because he wanted one, but then neglected them. Then again, maybe she wouldn't be so into someone with clear animal cruelty issues. We were only six when the hamster debacles happened, but still. I only killed one fish in my life and it was a result of me throwing fish food into Randy's face last year, which was one of the best events of my life, so I don't regret it.

"Oh. I was hoping for a better answer."

"I'm sorry. I don't have one. You know, my brother probably won't like you anymore if you spend too much time with me, so you should probably go."

"He doesn't seem like the jealous type."

"He's not. He'll just think you're an idiot for spending time with me." Just like Sophie apparently does.

"Well, I'm not sure I care that much what he thinks anymore."

～

It was Valentine's Day. Love was in the air. Well, except the air around my crew. Our airspace was filled mainly with loneliness, sorrow, and regret. I stood with Ben, Sammie, Luke, and Just Charles in the Atrium as cards, chocolates, flowers, and chocolate flowers were being handed out like candy, which of course, most of it was.

"This is the worst day ever," Just Charles said.

"Even worse than when Batman and Superman fought?" Luke asked.

"Definitely," I said. "The one dance we didn't try to mess with is totally messed up," I said.

"See? I told you we should've done something big with

it. Now, it's just a disaster. None of us have dates and your former dates hate you," Luke said, looking at me and Just Charles.

"Thanks for that," I said.

"Well, I'm still going," Just Charles said, puffing out his chest. "I'm gonna win her back."

"I'm still going," Ben said.

"You're crazy if you think I'm gonna let you dance with Allie all night," Luke said. "I'm going."

"Nothing's changed for me, so I'm in. I've always been going solo," Sammie said.

"Rub it in, please," I said.

"Sorry," Sammie said, hanging her head in shame. "Have you talked to her? What are you gonna do?"

"She said she didn't want to talk."

"She hasn't talked to me, either."

"You can still win the contest."

"I can't. Even if I win the Grand Gesture of Love, we still lose. We only got one point for the stupid obstacle course, Trust game."

"That was deserved," Luke said.

"Thanks," I said.

"So, do it anyway," Ben said.

"Yeah, show her you still care about her. Winning or losing the contest doesn't change that," Sammie said.

I nodded my head. I had nothing better to do and if there was a chance Sophie would be there, I didn't want to miss it. "One problem," I said. "How do we know she'll even show up?"

"Let me take care of that," Sammie said.

I shrugged. "I doubt she'll go, but okay. I have nothing to lose. I've already lost everything."

My crew didn't know what to say. Even Luke appeared to

feel bad.

The warning bell rang, so we departed to Advisory. As I headed to class with Just Charles and Luke, I saw Derek moping down the hallway. There was so much moping going on in school, I thought they might change our mascot from the Gophers to the Mopers. It would be an improvement, in my opinion.

"What's wrong with you?" I asked.

"I just broke up with Mia," he said.

"You broke up with her?" Based on my conversation with her, I thought he would have gotten dumped.

"It was mutual," he said, unconvincingly.

"Did you really like her that much?"

"Meh."

"So why are you upset?"

"Nobody likes to get dump- er, to break up." Derek shrugged. "I guess she was kind of weird. She went into this whole thing about hamsters. I had no idea what she was talking about."

So, maybe I told her.

Derek continued, "Where did she get the whole hamster thing?"

"I have no idea."

~

It was Friday night. The Valentine's Day dance was upon us. All of the craziness of the past few weeks was about to end. Would it end in disaster or triumph? I had no idea. Sophie had skipped lunch earlier in the day and sat with Dayna in science, leaving me alone at my lab table. I still didn't know if she would even show up.

I stared in the mirror, clipping on my best tie, and took a

deep breath. Going to a dance was stressful enough. True, I wasn't trying to save or ruin this one. But I had Cupid's Cutest Couple Contest to deal with and it was getting to me. I was supposed to present my Grand Gesture of Love to Sophie in front of everyone. And be judged. I had already been judged and dumped. I wondered if it would be better if Sophie didn't show up. Maybe Sammie hadn't convinced her yet.

I got to the dance early, with the hopes that there wouldn't be a lot of people there, but that one of them would be Sophie. Ben joined me, also hoping that he would beat Luke to the dance floor with Allie, if he had the guts to ask her.

Speaking of guts to ask, I saw Zorch pacing around the corner of the gym, seemingly talking to himself. I looked around to see Miss Geller talking to Mrs. Callahan on the other side of the gym.

Zorch looked up at me. "Oh, hey, buddy."

"What are you doing over here when Miss Geller is over there?"

"Trying to get up my nerve to ask her to dance."

"You already asked her. You gotta do it. You asked her to come here. She wanted to be here with you. You love her meatloaf. I think it's meant to be," I said, but not sure why.

"I'm sure a lot of guys love her meatloaf."

"I'm not as certain." I also wasn't certain that a love of someone's meatloaf was a strong foundation for a romantic relationship, but I was only a kid. Zorch didn't strike me as the type to all of a sudden become a vegan and destroy their romantic foundation, but still.

I turned around when I heard Ben yell, "That's it! I've had it with you!" He surged at Luke faster than I ever saw him move in his entire life. I think it caught Luke by surprise. Ben wrapped his arms around Luke's waist, his right shoulder jamming into Luke's gut. They tumbled to the ground in a heap of arms and legs, rolling over like a log as neither could gain an advantage. I think part of it was because neither of them actually knew what to do.

Mr. Muscalini rushed over, blowing his whistle like he was one of those super annoying kids who just got his first whistle and tries to kill people with it. "Rough housing! That'll get you each ten minutes in the penalty box!" He grabbed them with one arm each and pulled them apart like it was nothing. He probably did the same exercises with weights heavier than they were.

The dance was going downhill fast and it had barely started.

I turned to find Lionel and Kara standing next to me. I looked at Lionel and said, "Things are getting crazy."

"It's the full moon, man," Lionel said.

"Why does that have anything to do with it?"

"The full moon affects the tides, bro."

"And?"

"And our bodies are made up of seventy percent water. The full moon makes everyone wacky."

I was a science whiz and I had never heard that, but I guessed it could be true. I thought I might go crazy regardless, if Sophie didn't show up.

"What are you doing for your Grand Gesture?" I asked Lionel.

"A poem."

"You?"

"A song. If Sophie shows up. I don't even know if I want to. This contest is the worst thing that's happened to me since Randy moved here."

"Yeah, he's a real putz, dude."

I stood there with Lionel and Kara, not saying all that much, just surveying the scene. Ben and Luke were still in the penalty box. DJ Fight Club was on the scene, but no sign of Calvin or Devi. A few kids were on the dance floor. Zorch had made it halfway to Miss Geller, but was still talking to himself, while most of the kids were either standing against the wall or eyeing the refreshment table.

I watched as Mr. Muscalini patrolled the dance floor like a referee in the Super Bowl. He kept blowing his whistle at every infraction and calling out the penalty, "Illegal use of the hands, Finklestein. Lower back not upper butt."

"Hey, Miss Dawson. Illegal use of the lips to the face."

"Back it up over there, Hobbs. Offensive holding."

"That's a personal foul, Mr. Winslow. And you, Peralta, that's just terrible dancing. I feel my protein shake backing up on me." Mr. Muscalini started to wretch. "Ooh, it tastes like coconut. Not bad. Tastes about the same as the first time."

"Sir, that should be a big red flag," Blake Peralta said.

And then I saw her. Sophie walked in with Ditzy Dayna. I walked toward her, but then stopped. My heart was pounding. My mouth suddenly felt like Derek had shoved his dirty sock in my mouth (don't ask). I didn't know what to say to her.

She looked over at me. We stared at each other for a minute, neither of us moving. I so wanted everything to be back to normal. I rushed toward her, but she disappeared into a dancing pack of girls. I decided to follow. I wasn't giving up on Saustin that easily. I waded into the pack, never before having the courage to do it, motivated by my desire to get Sophie back. Amanda Gluskin almost grabbed me as she did the Cha Cha or something, but I did a spin move and kept going. I got through to the other side of the pack without harm, but never found Sophie. She was gone.

I scratched my head, as I stood on the edge of the dance floor. Just Charles walked up beside me.

"You seen Sophie?" I asked.

"Nah. I can't keep my eyes off Cheryl.

He pointed to Cheryl and Lincoln on the dance floor.

"I have an idea," he said.

He grabbed my arm and rushed over to Mr. Muscalini.

"What are you doing?" I asked.

"I need your help. Operation: Thwart Lincoln."

I had my own mission, but I couldn't let Just Charles down. He needed me.

When we got to Mr. Musacalini, Just Charles said, "Looks like Van Snoogle-Something and that troublemaker, Lincoln Madison, are racking up some major dance-floor violations."

Mr. Muscalini analyzed the dancing situation. He shook his head. "I'm not seeing it, Zaino. The elbows are locked out. Hands on the upper back. No smoochie smoochies. I can't do anything for you here."

"Please, for once, help me out. If you won't do it for me, do it for love."

"All right, Zaino. You hit me where it hurts."

Just Charles and I looked at each other, confused.

"I know what your middle school minds are thinking, but I was talking about my heart."

"Oh, right," I said.

"Yeah, we knew that," Just Charles scoffed.

Mr. Muscalini blew his whistle and stormed over to Cheryl and Lincoln. "You're offsides, Miss Van Snoogle-Something! Five-minute penalty. You'll have to sit the next song out."

"For what?" Cheryl said, confused.

"Don't question the coach," Mr. Muscalini said.

Just Charles smiled and said, "We gotta get Lincoln out of the picture."

"Who am I, John Wilkes Booth? Do you want me to take him outside and beat him up?"

"Do you think you could take him? I'm not so sure."

"Dude, I was joking. I'm not going to beat him up."

"Good, because I think you would lose."

"Yeah, you mentioned that," I said, annoyed. "I got my own problems to deal with."

"Please. Run some interference for me."

"Okay," I said, huffing. "What do you need?"

"A few minutes alone with Cheryl. I just need to talk to her."

"All right. I have an idea."

Cheryl and Lincoln stood about two feet apart as they

perused the beverage table. Just Charles slipped in between them.

"Oh, that looks lovely. I'm quite thirsty. How about you, Cheryl?"

Lincoln stared at Just Charles and pointed at Cheryl.

"Oh, am I in the way? Sorry," Just Charles said with a smile, but didn't move.

I stepped next to Lincoln on the opposite side and handed him a drink.

"Dude," I said to Lincoln, handing him a cup of water. "Drink up, man. Gotta stay hydrated. Dancing takes a lot out of you."

"Thanks," Lincoln said, glancing back at Cheryl. He drank a little bit.

"How about a little more?" I asked. I tipped the cup up from the bottom.

Lincoln guzzled the water. I held it there until he was finished. I grabbed another.

"Here, have some more."

"I'm good, man. Thanks."

"You probably have to pee now, right?"

"Nah, I'm fine," Lincoln said. "That's the first thing I've had since lunch."

It was not going exactly as I planned.

"Yeah, but the body is made up of 70% water. And the tides are wacky with the full moon."

"What does that have to do with anything?"

I had no idea, so I made something up. "It makes the water move through your system faster."

He wasn't buying it. Thankfully, someone walked up to the table to my right. I pretended he bumped into me. I jerked my hand toward Lincoln, spraying his shirt with the water in my cup.

"Oh, dude. Sorry!" I said.

"Ahh, that's okay." Lincoln looked around.

I didn't want him to spot the napkins at the end of the table. I grabbed his shoulder and ushered him toward the boys' locker room.

"Let's get you to the locker room to dry off."

"I'll be right back, Cheryl!" Lincoln called out.

I pushed Lincoln into the locker room and hustled back to Just Charles. I slipped in between Just Charles and Nick DeRozan, which was hard to do, because Nick took up half the table himself.

"So, umm, you know," Just Charles said.

Uh, oh. He was going blank, which I guess wasn't a huge surprise, because it was his last name, but he was usually better than Ben.

"I wanted to say," Just Charles continued, "that I'm, umm."

I leaned in and whispered, "Sorry."

"I'm sorry."

"Okay," Cheryl said.

"I like you," I whispered.

Just Charles turned to me and said, "I like you, too."

"Say it to her, idiot," I whispered.

Just Charles turned back to Cheryl. "I like you." And then thankfully, his brain started working a bit better. "I like you, like a lot. I was afraid you would break up with me. I just didn't think I could take that kind of rejection. So...I dumped you first. I know it's stupid, but..."

"It's not stupid," Cheryl said. "It's cute."

"It is?" Just Charles asked, surprised.

"Well, cute and stupid," Cheryl said. "And you really hurt my feelings. I liked you a lot, too."

"Liked?" Just Charles asked, nervously.

"Well, still do."

"Do you forgive me?"

I didn't even wait for her to answer. I saw Sophie across the dance floor and took off running.

25

I ran through the crowd, nearly losing my head from Brad Melon's wild dance moves. He was throwing more elbows than an MMA fight. And even threw in a Kung-Fu kick. When I got to the other side, Sophie was gone. I scanned the room and picked her out of the crowd. The chase was on. Again.

Sophie was playing a strong defense. She either disappeared or huddled with friends every time I tried to get close. She pretended I didn't exist. When I saw her at the edge of a pack of girls near the drink table, I slinked up around the outside, using my ninja skills. I carefully navigated the shadows, making my way closer to her. I slipped from one pack to another behind Nick DeRozan. And then did a dive roll behind another. I was only one pack away.

I looked around. I had no cover. I was going to have to break into open territory and risk detection to get near Sophie. I used my hand to block my eyes as I looked down at the ground, hoping she wouldn't see my face. I walked toward her. When I got there, I looked up. She was gone. There was jostling in the middle of a nearby group. I had seen that kind of jostling before. It was like the Nerd Herd during gym class. We used it to protect ourselves against the dodgeball. This time, I was the dodge ball, apparently.

I tried to pry Eva Davis and Wendy Grier apart, but I had no luck. They were Sophie's front line of defense.

"Sophie? Sophie, please! Are you even in there?" I stood on my tippy toes to see into the herd. "I see your curls. Just talk to me, please!"

"I don't want to talk to you!" Sophie called out. "Go away!"

Her words cut me deeper than any knife or sword could. I stood there for a second, not sure what to do.

Eva Davis pointed to the wall and said, "Go."

I hung my head in shame and slinked away. I found myself in between Ben and Luke in the penalty box.

"You get put in the penalty box, too?" Ben asked.

"Technically, no. But kinda yes. It's really more like the garbage pile."

"That bad, huh?" Luke asked.

"Pretty much," I said.

"I kinda feel the same," Ben said.

"Dude, what's up with you guys?" I asked them. "Why are you even fighting over Allie? She's just using you guys. She likes the attention."

And just as I said that, Allie started walking over to us.

"Oh, boy," I said.

"What?" Ben said, staring over at Sammie and Ditzy Dayna.

"Allie's headed this way."

"What?" Ben said, distracted.

I nudged him as Allie stood in front of him.

"Oh, hi," Ben said.

"You haven't asked me to dance," Allie said.

"Yeah, I guess I haven't," Ben said, glancing over at Sammie.

"Well? I told you I would save you a dance."

Ben looked at me, then at Sammie, and then back at Allie. I was starting to get confused.

Ben said, "I'm sorry, but I didn't save one for you."

Allie's mouth dropped open. My eyes bulged.

Ben continued, "Excuse me. I have to go do something."

Ben stood up, walked past Allie, and strode confidently toward Sammie.

I stood up and shrugged. "I gotta go. See you later." I walked away, watching Luke as I went. I wasn't sure what he would do.

Luke stood up, said something to Allie, and then walked over to the refreshment table, leaving her alone in the penalty box, which was kinda deserved.

I scanned the room for Ben. He stood in front of Sammie, his hand out for her to grab. She took his hand and then he led her to the dance floor. Both had huge smiles on their faces.

26

The adult relationships were seemingly going just as wacky as the kid ones. It was the full moon, or so I was told. Those pesky tides.

As I walked toward the refreshments table, I saw Mr. Muscalini mumbling to himself in the corner. First Zorch, now him. I walked over to Mr. Muscalini.

"What now?" I said. I was getting tired of all the drama.

"I kind of asked Ms. Pierre on a date."

"What?" I yelled.

"She's got power moves. I fell for her. Hard. There's nothing wrong with being attracted to a good, strong woman, Austin," he said, defensively.

"I suffer from the same problem, sir."

"She's my boss. What was I thinking?"

And she was mean and kinda scary, but I wasn't going to throw that in. "What happened?" I wasn't sure I wanted to know, but I didn't really have anything better to do.

"I told her that she was very mysterious. I didn't know what her relationship status was because everyone calls her Ms. She told me that she was single."

"I tried that, too. She didn't tell me, though."

"You asked Ms. Pierre out?" Mr. Muscalini asked, puffing out his enormous chest.

"No, sir. I just wanted to know if she was single so I could set her up with someone and not be so focused on giving me detention. Carry on."

Mr. Muscalini said, "After she told me she was single, I said, 'Well, then I swipe left.'"

"I don't know what that means, sir."

He ignored me. "Davenport, I give you full authority to have the entire dance pummel me with dodge balls."

"I can't do that, sir. You're just gonna have to suck it up and get back on the field. The team is counting on you!"

"You're right! Wait, what team?"

"Your team!"

Mr. Muscalini ran off screaming, like he was going to war. I wasn't sure where he was going or what he was going to do there, but he was really pumped about it.

I continued my walk, headed across the dance floor, and did a double take. "Mr. Gifford?"

Mr. Gifford stood before me. His beard was cleanly shaven. There were no remnants of any meals on his face. He looked like a new man.

"Good evening, Austin," Mr. Gifford said, cheerfully.

"Sir, what happened?" I said. "I mean that in a good way."

"I'm a little embarrassed to say this. Not sure if you'll think I'm crazy, but do you know Max Mulvihill, by any chance?"

"Do I? Of course, I do. He's helped me and Ben out a bunch."

"Oh, good. I kinda thought I was a little crazy, like it was too good to be true."

"Join the club."

"I did. I don't like the idea of paying to poop, but he runs a real nice place."

"What happened?"

"I realized something important. I need to learn to love me before I can truly love another. I'm going lone wolf for a while."

"Lone wolf without the beard?"

"I think so."

"That's good news, sir." I think.

Zorch walked up and joined our conversation.

"What are you doing here? Did you ask Miss Geller to dance?"

"Not yet, but..."

I was done with this nonsense. "But...no. I didn't want to have to tell you this, but I think I'm gonna have to. Have you ever seen the movie Back to the Future?"

"Yes. It's a classic."

"Do you remember when Calvin Conklin thought I was a time traveler?"

"Yes."

"Well, I've denied it, up until now. But it's true. You see, I'm from the future. And if you don't get out there and ask her to dance, well, I might never exist. I'm your son." I pretended to be woozy. "I feel my particles evaporating as we speak."

Zorch looked at me and took off running toward Miss Geller.

I looked up at Mr. Gifford and smiled. "Works every time."

"This is incredible!" Mr. Gifford said. He grabbed me by the shoulders. "I need to borrow the time machine. I have to fix things with Mrs. Funderbunk. And if that doesn't work, buy some lottery tickets."

Oh, geez. I thought Max had cured him. But I didn't have time to worry about that. I saw Ben and Sammie holding hands, talking to Sophie.

"It's in the shop," I said. "Problems with the flux capacitor. Not generating enough gigiwatts."

"Makes sense," Mr. Gifford said.

I rushed off, using my ninja skills once again to disappear into the shadows. I slinked around a small group of giggling girls and slipped in between Ben and Sophie.

"Please, listen to me before you run away..." I said, as Sophie ran away. I continued anyway, talking to myself, "How's it going? Good? You look pretty."

I shook my head and walked away.

27

Mr. Muscalini was back at his pity party. Apparently, I needed to give him more guidance. He paced around the outside of the dance floor, seemingly distressed. And talking to himself, of course. As I walked by, he looked up at me.

"Davenport, do you think it's worse for your life to be ruined or in shambles?"

I shrugged.

He looked up at the ceiling. "What did I do?"

"Don't worry, sir. Everybody is a little wacky. It's the full moon."

Mr. Muscalini twisted his body to look at his butt. "My rock-solid glutes didn't make me do any of this. But they could win the game!" he said, excitedly. "I'm gonna walk by Ms. Pierre. See if she checks out my butt."

"I can't do that, sir." Things got weird, fast.

"Davenport, please! I'm begging you."

"I gotta go, sir," I said, walking off.

Jimmy Trugman was standing at the edge of the dance floor. I headed over toward him. I had nothing better to do.

"What's up, nerd?" I asked.

"Just being a nerd," Jimmy said. "Trying to figure out who to ask to dance and then just standing here. Does this ever get easier?"

I looked over at Mr. Gifford, Mr. Muscalini, and Zorch and said, "I don't think so, bro."

"I figured that," he said.

"Hey, Jimmy, I think Frannie Pearson's got her eye on you."

"Yeah?" Jimmy looked onto the dance floor to see Frannie Pearson standing off to the side of the dance floor with a few girls, all of them looking longingly at the other girls dancing.

"Absolutely." I actually had no idea. She had barely looked in our direction, but the dude needed to take a chance.

"Ask her to dance," I said, like it was so easy to do. I didn't even know why I was setting everyone up when I knew it would just end in disaster.

"I think I will," Jimmy said, smiling, and then headed across the dance floor.

❧

IT WAS time for my least favorite part of the night: the conclusion to the Cupid's Cutest Couple Contest.

DJ Fight Club cut the music as Devi Divine and Calvin Conklin made their way to the stage. Thankfully, Calvin was dressed somewhat normally, with jeans and a sweater filled with hearts. It wasn't the best shirt, but at least he was wearing a shirt. And not a diaper.

Calvin took the microphone from DJ Fight Club and said, "Thank you, Miss Fight Club. It's now time for the

Grand Gesture of Love and then to name Cupid's Cutest Couple!"

The crowd cheered. I searched everywhere for Sophie, but couldn't find her.

Devi said, "That's right, Calvin. And this contest has had no shortage of twists and turns. Let's get everybody up to speed on where things stand."

"It's been a battle, but the field clearly separated getting to this point. Randy and Regan sit in first place with their solid interview and powerful performance at the couple's game night. I'd like to invite Randy up to the stage for his Grand Gesture of Love!" Calvin yelled.

Randy strode confidently to the stage. He took the microphone from Calvin. Devi and Calvin walked over to the DJ booth. Randy took a deep breath and nodded at DJ Fight Club.

I thought Randy would sing his Love Puddle song, "Together Forever", but since he and Regan had broken up twice already in the eight months they had known each other, maybe he realized that wasn't a good call.

Randy said, "Tonight, I'm launching my solo career. I've left Love Puddle behind. I've outgrown them like Davenfart has outgrown those pants, but doesn't seem to know it. The rest of Love Puddle just wasn't as talented as me."

A bunch of people started cheering. Even Nick started clapping.

I didn't like the insult, but I was at least thankful he noticed I was growing.

"Weren't you in the band?" I asked Nick.

He took a menacing step toward me. I jumped back and immediately wondered if I should check my underwear. I clenched my butt cheeks and realized I was good.

Randy continued, "I wrote this myself. This is called, "I

know why you love me" and it's gonna be a huge hit." Randy stood in the center of the stage, his head down. "DJ Fight Club- hit it!"

The music started playing. It was a slow jam. Randy followed with his signature dance moves. If I had to give him some credit, he was a great dancer. Still, I hoped he would trip and fall off the stage.

Randy looked down at Regan who stood at the bottom of the stage, surrounded by a bunch of screaming girls. DJ Fight Club shone a spotlight on her. Randy started singing, "Girl, you don't have to try, to say that you love me, 'cause I know you do. And here's why."

The pace of the music kicked up three notches as Randy continued singing, "I'm the quarterback of the team, I'm in every girl's dreams. I got smokin' dance moves and the most expensive shoes."

"This is a disaster," Ben said.

"This is terrible," Sammie added. "I think he missed the point. It's not supposed to be a grand gesture of love to himself."

Randy did a spin move and then ran his fingers down his cheek. "I've got this porcelain skin. I know how to win. My perfect hair. These eyes. Are just some of the reasons why. You love me. I know you do. And I know you know, I'm numero uno."

Randy raised the microphone into the air as the music trailed off. He looked around, not sure why the whole place wasn't going crazy. The look on his face was priceless.

Somehow, though, Regan thought it was amazing. She was clapping and jumping up and down. The only other person in the room who showed any enthusiasm for his Grand Gesture of Love was Senora Fuentes, who was probably just excited because he put some Spanish in his song.

Somebody in the crowd yelled out, "Go back to Love Puddle. You stink!" It may have been Mr. Gifford. He followed with, "Wait! They stink, too!"

Calvin stepped forward, unsure. He took the microphone from Randy and said, "You can't win 'em all, kid. Have a seat."

Randy slumped off the stage. Regan rushed to him and engulfed him in a hug.

Calvin said, "Well, that was interesting. I've seen train wrecks with happier endings. Haven't you, Devi?"

"No," she said, shaking her head. "Before Randy's performance, in second place, we had Lionel and Kara, who gave a great interview and won the Newlywed Game."

"That was quite the performance for the couple, who have only been together a few short months," Calvin said.

"Lionel is going to recite a poem."

Lionel walked up onto the stage to some cheers and then

took the microphone from Calvin. His hands shook, as he held it up in front of his face, which seemed to morph three shades lighter just as he stood there. Lionel gulped as he looked out into the crowd.

All signs pointed to bombing. The crowd gasped.

"What's happening?" I asked Ben and Sammie.

"He's always so smooth," Ben said. "So laid back."

Ben was right. Lionel was a surfer. He just went with the flow. There was only one answer as to what was happening. Sabotage! Lionel wretched and covered his mouth. He dropped the mic and rushed to the back of the stage. And hurled like he had just swallowed a monsoon and couldn't hold it down. A monsoon with the school's worst batch of seafood surprise ever created.

The crowd groaned with each 'Hwulah' and there were a lot of them. I'm a smart dude and I lost count after twenty-six. Randy and Regan were going to win the contest. I almost joined Lionel in the puke fest.

28

L ionel jumped off the stage and rushed past us and into the locker room. I followed him. I guess I wanted to see him puke more.

When I caught up to him, I asked, "Are you okay? What happened?"

Lionel patted some water on his face and said, "I think I ate something funky."

"What was it?" Ben asked.

"I grabbed some tacos from Tony Tequila's. It was spicier than usual, but I didn't think anything about it."

"Where did you eat it?"

"Here. In the Atrium before the dance started. I was running late."

"Did it taste like cayenne pepper?" That was Randy's go-to cheating spice. Yes, he had a cheating spice. That's how much he cheated. He used cayenne pepper to make himself cry in our crying contest back during the Santukkah! Musical rehearsals. And I used it to make him puke, unfortunately, during the first night of the actual musical.

"Yeah, it did kinda taste like cayenne. I think they gave me the spicy even though I asked for medium."

"I'm not so sure. Did you leave the food unattended at any time?"

"No, dude. Why?"

I was deflated. "I thought Randy sabotaged you, but I guess it was just bad luck."

"Why would he do that?" Lionel asked.

"Because he's a cheater," Ben said.

"Ahhh, man. I asked Regan to watch my food because I had to run to the bathroom."

"They sabotaged you," I said, simply. "You can't let him beat you. You gotta get back out there, man."

"I can't. I just puked in front of the whole school, dude."

"Yeah, that was pretty bad, bro," Ben said.

"Not helping, Benjamin," I said.

I didn't know what to say. If he didn't get back out there, I had a better shot at winning, but I couldn't let Randy win by cheating. I actually had no idea if I could still win the contest, since Sophie broke up with me.

"I can't disappoint Kara, but I can't go back out there."

I remembered Lionel's interview speech. I grabbed him by the shoulders and looked up at him. I said, "Sometimes you ride a wave into the sunset. Sometimes you eat sand. Get back on the board, dude! Ride the wave!"

"Yeah!" Lionel yelled.

I slapped him on his back, which proved to be a bad idea, as he wretched and hurled again into the sink.

"Nice one, Aus," Ben said.

"You okay?" I asked.

"I think so, just don't touch me."

"Roger that, bro. Now get out there!"

Ben and I followed Lionel back out into the gym. We

stopped at the bottom of the stage as Lionel headed up the stairs.

Calvin looked Lionel up and down and took a step back from him. "Well, after seeing what just happened out here, we have no desire to know what happened in there. So, let's continue like none of that just happened."

"Gladly," Lionel said. He smiled at the crowd. I think he may have had regurgitated taco on his tooth, but it was too late to do anything about it at that point.

Lionel grabbed the microphone and looked over at Kara, who was off to the side of the stage. My poem is called, 'Waves of Love.' I rise out of bed, to see your smile that shines like the morning sun, giving me hope for the day ahead. Your touch, familiar so, like warm sand in my toes."

I looked over at Kara, who was giggling like crazy. I think that's all she was capable of doing when in Lionel's presence.

Lionel continued, "I love your cute nose. It wiggles when you giggle and it makes my heart jiggle. But there are times when sadness fills my heart. For it weeps when we're apart. My love for you spans the world's oceans. It protects me like 50 SPF lotion. I will love you to the end of days until I float to the heavens above. Until then, let's ride the waves of love."

Mr. Muscalini burst into sobs and grabbed Derek, wrapping him in a giant bear hug. "That was beautiful." My brother looked like he was gonna puke, too.

Kara rushed up onto the stage and into Lionel's arms. Everyone was cheering. Well, until they started kissing and everyone realized that he had just puked his intestines out just a few minutes prior.

People were running left and right, hurling in garbage pails and flower pots. I'm not sure anybody was keeping track, but I'm sure we set some dozens of Guinness Book of World Records including the most puke ever regurgitated at a school event and the most people puking concurrently.

After a ten-minute break, the contest was back on. Cupid's Cutest Couple Contest was hard core. It was like the Marines of couple contests.

Calvin stood next to Devi and said, "Well, this has certainly been interesting. I've been informed by my invisible friend, Ted, that even though everyone is completely disgusted, we are to judge Lionel's poem without the puking." Calvin grabbed his earpiece, "We're certain the puking wasn't part of the romantic gesture? No, Ted. My mother did not drop me on my head when I was a baby. Should I ask her?"

Devi interrupted, "So, that means, Lionel crushed that round. It's going to be difficult for any of the remaining participants to catch the leaders."

Ugh. I had a lot of work to do. Sophie and me, if there still was a Sophie and me, were in third place. My Grand Gesture of Love was gonna have to be the grandest. And it was my time. I didn't have any idea if Sophie was still even there, let alone if we would be together after this, but I was going to fight for us in the contest.

"Let's continue!" Calvin said. "I think we all want to move on. Devi, get us up to speed because, frankly, I'm so grossed out, I don't really have any idea what's going on."

"I think that's pretty much all the time, but let's move on! We're ready for our next Grand Gesture of Love. And in third place," Devi said, "we have Ditzy, er Dayna and Brad!"

Wait, what?

"This just in," Calvin said, holding his earpiece like he was giving his newscast. "We have just been informed that Sophie and Austin have backed out of the competition! That makes two couples out!"

"You're actually right, Calvin. By process of elimination, you can probably figure out that Derek and Mia have also left the contest."

"I heard Derek got dumped," Calvin said.

"It was mutual!" Derek yelled from the crowd.

The crowd groaned and chattered in surprise. My heart dropped. I knew things weren't looking good, but I at least had hope that I could fix it. That hope was gone. Sophie must have withdrawn us from the contest.

Ben said, "What just happened? Why are you out?"

"I don't know. I guess Sophie quit. I have to find her," I said, taking off.

I searched the packed gym, but couldn't find her anywhere. I don't know why, but Sophie pulling out of the contest hurt almost as bad as her breaking up with me.

I saw Zorch standing next to Miss Geller. I didn't really want to talk to him, but he was taller than everybody in the room, so I thought he might be able to scout out Sophie for me.

"Have you seen Sophie?" I asked.

"Not for a while, buddy. Everything okay?"

I looked up at him. "Take it from me, Zorch," I said, wiping a tear out of my eye. "Live. Love. You never know when it'll all just fade into blackness, like my brother's butt chin."

"That's deep, Austin."

"That's what I'm trying to tell you. Take this young lady," I grabbed Miss Geller's hands and put them into Zorch's. "And hold on for as long as you can. You're two beautiful souls. You love her terrible meatloaf," I said. "If that's not a sign you should be together, I don't know what is."

I walked away. Both of them were scratching their heads. I circled the gym and made it back to my crew, Sophie nowhere to be found.

"I'm out."

"Where are you going?" Ben asked.

"I'm leaving. Going to drown my sorrows in pizza at Frank's. Sophie dumped me and backed out of the contest without even telling me. We're finished. There's no coming back from that."

"You're just giving up?" Ben asked.

"She refuses to talk to me," I said. "I don't even know if she's still here."

"I'll find her," Sammie said. "She's probably in the girls' bathroom."

"I knew I should've gone in there," I said.

"Yeah, it's probably better that you didn't," Ben said.

"I'll see you in a few minutes," Sammie said, smiling at Ben.

"I can't wait!" I called after her.

"She was talking to me," Ben said, happily.

"I know. I don't know why I'm sticking around."

"Because you still want to be with Sophie."

"True. But I don't know what to do about it."

"Do the Grand Gesture of Love? It's obvious, bro."

"Oh, now you're the love doctor?" I asked, smirking.

"Do you need a Muscalini motivational speech?"

"Hard pass," I said. "I'm not in the mood."

"Get in the mood. This is your time. Would Harry Potter give up against Voldemort?"

"Never!" I yelled, and then thought for a moment. "Is Sophie Voldemort? Upon reflection, I'm not sure I like this analogy."

"No. The situation is Voldemort."

"How am I going to do the Grand Gesture of Love? I'm out of the contest."

"Get yourself back in. Dude, this is all stuff you should know."

"You may not want motivation by Muscalini, but how about I give you my best Hagrid impression?"

"Umm, I'll go up there if you promise not to do it."

"That 'urts," Ben said with his best Hagrid impersonation.

"Watch it," I said, steeling my nerve. I took a deep breath and walked toward the stairs.

"You're a wizard, Harry!"

I ignored Ben and tried not to laugh as I walked up the steps. Calvin and Devi were nowhere to be found. I guessed they were taking a break before announcing the winner of the contest. The microphone they shared lay across the shelf on top of DJ Fight Club's booth. I thought about grabbing it and just going for it, but DJ Fight Club looked like a reasonable woman. I decided to get her blessing first.

I walked up next to the booth. DJ Fight Club was a good deal taller than me. She was lanky with brown hair pulled back into a pony tail and wore headphones atop her head.

"I'm not taking any requests," she said, barely looking at me.

"I'm not requesting a song. I, well, I think there's been a mistake. Calvin said that I pulled out of the contest, but I didn't. I still need to perform my Grand Gesture."

"You're Austin?"

"Yes," I said, crossing my fingers behind my back.

"Yeah, Sophie quit. She told me herself."

I nodded, taking it all in. "I still want to do it. I need to do it."

"Sorry, you're out," DJ Fight Club said without a care.

I looked down into the crowd to see Sophie standing next to Sammie at the bottom of the stage. I was so excited to see her. And you know, not protected by a herd of catty chicks determined to ruin my life. She didn't look overly happy to be there, but still, she was there.

I looked back at DJ Fight Club. "Please, I need to win her back."

"She obviously doesn't want to be won back. Now, get off my stage."

I stood there and stared at DJ Fight Club. It was my stage. I won this dance for Sophie and I wasn't going to take 'no' for an answer. I nodded at DJ Fight Club and headed back around the DJ booth. I grabbed the mic off the shelf and flipped it on.

I cleared my throat, ninja-walked over to the edge of the stage, and sang over the music, "Sophie, don't ya know me? Look into my eyes, and you'll see. Don't believe the lies. Please don't do this to me." I was making it up as I went along. I had written a different song before she dumped me.

I looked at her. She looked angry or maybe confused.

I continued, "I feel like a chump. It don't feel good to get dumped."

Sophie yelled back at me, "I didn't dump you! You dumped me!"

Huh?

Before I could process what Sophie said, Sammie yelled, "Look out!"

Everyone was pointing behind me. I turned and saw DJ Fight Club soaring through the air before she rammed into me.

All I had time to do was widen my eyes, which was not really all that helpful in defending myself against the impending attack. She hit me harder than the 44 Blast (a football play the ferocious Gophers ran) and knocked me to the floor.

I tried to continue my song, "Sophie, you're the best thing that's ever happened to me-"

DJ Fight Club knocked the microphone from my hand and forced her weight down onto my back.

"No!" I yelled.

But it was too late. I winced in pain. DJ Fight Club slipped her thin fingers underneath my chin from both sides and interlocked them with fluidity. She had done it before. Perhaps many times. I guess with the name, DJ Fight Club, I shouldn't have been surprised. I struggled, but it was all for naught. DJ Fight Club had me in her clutches. The Camel Clutch to be exact. The most-deadly wrestling move ever designed. I mean, how many other wrestling moves can turn you into a camel? None. That's how many. I gasped for air. There may have been love in the air, but I was pretty certain there was no actual oxygen in the air. I looked at Sophie through hazy vision and then it all went black.

29

After Nurse Nova woke me up with smelling salts and perhaps a few slaps to the face (it was stinging), I saw Sophie staring at me with tears in her eyes. She rushed to me. My back ached as she squeezed me. One would think that my body would be used to the Camel Clutch by now, but I guess it is so devastating that despite the resilience of the human body and spirit, the Camel Clutch is just too overwhelmingly powerful.

"What happened?" I moaned. "What do you mean, 'I broke up with you?'" I asked. "If you haven't figured out that you're the only girl for me, then I don't know what to tell you. Although, you might want to work on controlling your competitiveness."

"Funny," Sophie said, smirking. "But you did break up with me. I got a note from you in my locker."

"It wasn't from me."

Ben rushed over. "I showed her the note that you texted to me."

Sophie said, "That's not my handwriting. I didn't break

up with you, either." She grabbed Ben's phone and showed me. I don't write my Gs or Ss like that."

My brain started aching like the rest of my body. "Did somebody try to break us up?" And then it all became clear. Every S jumped off the page at me. "I've seen those Ss before. But where?"

I looked at my crew, which was now fully assembled with Luke, Just Charles, and Sammie having arrived.

And then my run-in with Emily Springer popped into my head. The S from her initial popped into my mind. It had the same curl to it that Sophie's signature had on the breakup letter.

"Anybody seen Emily Springer?" I asked.

"Why?" Sophie asked.

"Because she has some explaining to do."

Sammie said, "But she's totally crazy for Randy. We used to talk about him when-" When she used to like him.

Ben looked at Sammie and she stopped talking.

"Why would she try to break us up?" Sophie asked.

"Maybe Randy put her up to it," Just Charles said. He was holding hands with Cheryl, in case you were wondering.

"But what about the whole contest conspiracy?" Cheryl asked. "I can dig into it if you want. Write an expose. I think this runs deeper. Could be all the way to the top."

"How could something run deeper all the way to the top?" Luke asked.

"You know what I mean," Cheryl said.

"Do you want me to dump him?" Just Charles asked. Cheryl shot lasers at him from her eyes. "Too soon?" He studied her face. "Yep. Too soon."

"Guys, I don't really care if it was Randy, Butt Hair, Ms.

Pierre or Big Foot." I looked at Sophie and smiled. "Contest. No contest. It doesn't matter."

Sophie squeezed my hand and smiled back.

Zorch walked up to our group, all smiles. It was good to see him happy.

"Austin, can I borrow you for a second?"

"Umm, sure," I said. I walked over to him.

"Thank you, buddy. I really appreciate what you've done for me. I never could've done this without you."

Yeah, that was pretty obvious. I smiled and said, "I've got a feeling about you two." I mean, if he loved her meatloaf, she could do no wrong.

And then Randy's voice called out from behind me, "Please, don't do this."

I turned around to see Regan storming off with Randy watching, just a few feet behind me.

Randy continued, "Regan, wait! Please! Oh, not again!" He ran his fingers through his hair. "She's dumped me three times," he whined.

I looked at Zorch with a smile and said, "Oh, how sweet it was to hear those words. They will forever echo in my brain. I will remember them during my darkest hours and they will bring joy to my heart."

"Shut your face, Davenfart!" Randy yelled.

Zorch nodded to something behind me. I turned around, expecting Randy to be in the midst of delivering a knuckle sandwich to my face. Sophie was standing in front of me.

"I'll catch you later, bud," Zorch said.

I barely heard what he said.

"Do you wanna dance?" she asked.

"There's no music."

"I'll sing to you, with my superior voice," Sophie said, smiling and holding out her hand.

I wasn't about to argue with her about my fabulous voice. I grabbed her hand and wrapped my arm around her back. I wasn't sure where Mr. Muscalini was at that moment, but I was solidly following all of his rules.

We started the typical middle school dance style, swaying back and forth.

"You don't have to sing," I said. "This is perfect."

"I'm sorry," she said. "I was so crazed about winning."

"I know," I said. "That same competitive side saved my life when you suction-cupped an arrow to Randy's forehead at the Medieval Renaissance Fair, so I can't get too angry."

"You should be angry. I was a jerk."

Was I supposed to agree with that? I didn't want to say anything that could mess up our already fragile relationship.

Thankfully, Sophie continued, "I just wanted all those cool things. The limo ride. The concert. Le Fart."

"You said it, not me," I said, laughing.

"I knew you would like that," Sophie said.

"Well, why can't we?"

"Can't what?"

"Get all those things?"

"How are we gonna get the money to do all that?"

"Well, I remember that Goat Turd owes us one. We did make them famous. And maybe they'll send us to the Caribbean or something. I need a vacation. Remember when you asked me what I wanted to be when I grew up? Well, I realized it's not a relationship counselor."

"But you're pretty good at it. I just love how you'll do anything for the people you care about."

"I am amazing like that."

"Don't push your luck," Sophie said, laughing.

The good news about slow dancing with the girl of your dreams with no music is that the song never ends.

Well, it ends when Mr. Muscalini blasts your ear with a whistle because the dance is over and you're in his gym. Did the guy sleep there or something? The whacko.

Well, that about wraps up this love story like a present in a bow. True, it reeks of farts and puke, but it still looks nice.

I'm sorry that this wasn't a storybook romance with a happily ever after. Most love stories don't happen in middle school or during a full moon. And don't include me and the mayhem that I seem to attract. And I think most love stories are worse for it.

If you're not that into love stories, just wait until you hear my detective story.

COMING SOON!

4/15/2020   6/15/2020

Education: Domestication- 8/15/2020

Class Tripped- 9/15/2020

Graduation Detonation- 11/15/2020

Got Audio?

Want to listen to Middle School Mayhem?

ABOUT THE AUTHOR

C.T. Walsh is the author of the Middle School Mayhem Series, set to be a total twelve hilarious adventures of Austin Davenport and his friends.

Besides writing fun, snarky humor and the occasionally-frequent fart joke, C.T. loves spending time with his family, coaching his kids' various sports, and successfully turning seemingly unsandwichable things into spectacular sandwiches, while also claiming that he never eats carbs. He assures you, it's not easy to do. C.T. knows what you're thinking: this guy sounds complex, a little bit mysterious, and maybe even dashingly handsome, if you haven't been to the optometrist in a while. And you might be right.

C.T. finds it weird to write about himself in the third person, so he is going to stop doing that now.

You can learn more about C.T. (oops) at ctwalsh.fun

 facebook.com/ctwalshauthor

ALSO BY C.T. WALSH

Down with the Dance: Book One

Santukkah!: Book Two

The Science (Un)Fair: Book Three

Battle of the Bands: Book Four

Medieval Mayhem: Book Five

The Takedown: Book Six

Future Release schedule

The Comic Con: April 15th, 2020

Election Misdirection: June 15th, 2020

Education: Domestication: August 15th, 2020

Class Tripped: September 15th, 2020

Graduation Detonation: November 15th, 2020

Made in the USA
Monee, IL
10 November 2020

47163635R00128